OLD MAN SMITHERS

LIZARDVILLE SIDE STORIES BOOK 2

OLD MAN SMITHERS

STEVE ALTIER

DEDICATION

Kim Gunn, thank you for everything.
I'm proud of you.

CONTENTS

ONE

Sunday, October 15, 1961

The lights blinded me as I crested the top of the hill. I panicked. "Bob!" April's screams pierced my eardrums. My son wailed in the back seat. I pressed my foot to the brake pedal and held it as hard as possible. Tires squealed as I white-knuckled the steering wheel to the right, trying to avoid the oncoming car. Everything slowed, and my life flashed before my eyes. The steering wheel pushed the air from my lungs. I glanced to the right, watching my wife fly forward. The crunching noise of her hitting the metal dashboard of our 1961 Dodge Dart sent chills down my spine. Glass and metal flew, and everything closed in around me. Screams turned to cries, then sobs, before fading to silence.

My nose twitched, and I caught a whiff of something horrible. *Wait, wait. No, it couldn't be.* Panic set in. I squirmed yet couldn't move. *Oh no, gas!* The scent was strong. I need to get out of here. I blinked. *How long had I been out?* My vision was stained. Everything was red. *Why was it red?* I was confused and in agony. Pain seared throughout my body. I raised my right hand slightly to wipe the debris from my eye. My finger bled. *A fresh cut? I must have a piece of glass embedded in my eyelid.* Confused, I tried to move my head to the right, but metal debris was scattered and restricted my movement. *April, where was April?* I needed to see her blonde hair. I couldn't move. My heart raced. Something held me in place. My stomach whirled. I wanted to throw up. The smell was strong. "April!" I shouted but heard nothing. *Was I dreaming? Lights.* I remembered the lights. *They were coming right at me as I crested the hill.*

I turned the steering wheel. I know I turned... or tried to turn. Did I turn too late? Water flowed from my eyes and burned when it mixed with the cuts on my face. What had I done? "April!" I screamed again. Silence. Was I yelling? Was I even talking? Was this all happening in my mind? Could I talk? I moved my lips and said, "Hello." I heard nothing.

I couldn't move. I tried to push with my feet, but my legs were pinned. I wiggled my toes. I could feel that. I smiled, then noticed the gift wrap—birthday wrapping, to be exact. *My son's birthday.* "Bobby!" I screamed. "Bobby Junior!" I coughed, sobbed, choked on my saliva, and sobbed some more. *Why was no one responding to me?* "Bobby? April? Is anyone there?" I couldn't even hear myself. My body hurt all over. I was dazed and confused. My mind whirled. *Was I alive? Was this the afterlife they talked about in church? Is that all I remembered from church? Was I a horrible person? So bad that I had been sentenced to an eternity in a pile of wrecked metal? I needed to be more sociable and treat people better. Please give me another chance!* I heard my mind scream as I faded.

I heard a voice. I thought I heard a voice. A man's voice grew louder. A bright light shone in my eye. *No, I* sobbed. *Not again. Not another car.* My mind was in a frenzy. "April? Bobby? Can you hear me?" *Where were my wife and son?* I needed to help them. I couldn't move. I was helpless. "Help my wife and son, please! Please!" My words fell silent as I drifted off.

"He's alive." His rough hands touched my neck, and I could feel his cold fingers. "Hun, get in the car, return to the gas station, and call for help. I'll stay here," the voice echoed.

"Wait?" I choked out, my voice tattered. *Was he gone? How could he leave me?* I drifted off. *Did the car move? Was something happening? Was the car moving? Was someone trying to pry the door open? No, it wasn't my door. Wait. It was coming from the other side of the car. Yes, yes.* I smiled on the inside. *They were helping April. Or even better, they were helping Bobby.* I knew they were going to be all right. Help had arrived.

A horrible thought filled my mind. *How would April take care of the house without me? Even worse, how was she going to pay the bills? With Todd, the guy at the body shop?* My mind was playing tricks on me. *He went to the gym all the time and worked out. He was tall and handsome, and he constantly flirted with April.* My blood boiled. *He flirted with all the pretty girls, and he was a playboy. She never said how she felt about him. Why was that? Thinking back, she never stopped him, either—please, April, not Todd.*

Wait, my cousin, Tom, could help. He was a distant cousin but a great guy and close friend. He spent all his time working and very little time enjoying life. Yes, he was single and could help April and Bobby. But he had dedicated his life to running the General Store. In a way, he was like me, a loner— all work and no play. My mind bounced around like a ping-pong ball. *Was anyone out there? Please don't leave.*

Bobby was learning how to bowl. He was a natural. Tonight, he rolled a 96. That's his highest game to date. Would he ever have a chance to hit 100 or even get a shot at beating me? Maybe one day. Would he ever get a chance to play for the little league baseball team? This year was his third time trying out and the third time he didn't make the team. Maybe I should have helped him more. He also had other interests, schoolwork, and books to read. He loved the Dracula *books. When he was a little older, I would take him to the movie show so he can watch* Dracula *on the big screen.*

I sobbed. *What if my boy never walked again? How would he ever bowl or play baseball? How could I have done this to my family? Am I the worst husband and father in town? Did I need a new car? Or a lovely house on the river? I don't know. Now, I wish I had not worked all those double shifts. I wish I had spent more time with Bobby playing catch or teaching him to swing the bat the correct way. But I was always too tired from working all the time. Why would I volunteer to work late and agree to come in on Saturdays? Why were money and material things so important to me?*

Lately, things had been going great—perfect, to be exact. That's it. That had to be it. Things were too good to be true. Just when you thought life was great, you got knocked down again.

I lost all feeling in my body. *Was everything shutting down? My mind was still working. At least, I thought it was still working. What would they write about me in the paper? Would anyone go to my funeral? Would I come back as a cat or dog? Some people believed that stuff. Would I come back as a ghost? I guess you would have to believe in ghosts before returning as one.* My thoughts bounced as I drifted in and out.

My left eye opened, and I saw a piece of metal blocking my view. I tried to look over it and around it with no luck. Pain flowed through every inch of my body. I guess it was good that I could feel pain. *Voices!* I heard male voices in the distance, several of them. I opened my eyes wider, trying to see what was happening outside this crumpled pile of metal. Everything was tinted red, but I noticed flashing red lights. There appeared to be more than one. Help had finally arrived. "Save April and Bobby first," I begged. But no one heard me. *My hearing seemed fine, so why had I not heard April or Bobby?* The car jerked back and forth a time or two. Finally, the door popped open, and I saw a man's face surrounded by the night sky. "He's alive," the voice whispered. "I have a survivor!" he yelled.

What did he mean, a survivor? No, no, there had to be more than one. April or Bobby had to be alive. They couldn't be… No, no, please, they'd done nothing wrong. My mind fluttered. Take me. This was my fault, not April's or Bobby's.

I thought of the other car. *What about the driver? Had they survived the crash? Oh no, what if he had a family like mine? What if his wife and children were in the car? What if it was someone I knew? After all, I worked at the car dealership and knew most people in town. Considering this was a little town in the middle of nowhere, how could I not know them all?* My head wanted to explode. I was pinned and trapped inside my car. I didn't know what was happening around me. The unknown was killing me. *Or… did I die in the accident?*

Wait, the male voice said I was alive. I think he was talking about me. "Relax." My heart rate slowed. "Please take a deep breath." I inhaled, and it burned. I coughed and tried to calm down. I needed to stay positive.

Voices gathered, and I felt pressure on my legs and arms. They tugged, pushed, and pulled. Piece by piece, the debris was removed. I had no idea how long I had been trapped when I heard the siren blare as the ambulance pulled away. I breathed a sigh of relief. *I knew April or Bobby were on their way to get medical attention. It had to be April and Bobby. It just had to be them.* My eyelids fluttered, and everything went murky.

"Be careful with his leg. Steady now." The voice was stern and focused. I floated upward; goosebumps popped up on my arm as the wind flowed past. "Easy, boys. Set him down on the board," he instructed. I felt something press my ankles to the hard surface, then my waist and chest, and last, my forehead.

"Okay, everyone, ready? Lift!" I rose a little higher. My eyes blinked in and out. "Give him oxygen." I felt something on the back of my head, and then a cup was placed over my mouth and nose.

I gasped as oxygen filled my lungs. I panted briefly and gulped in as much as possible. The stars appeared brighter, and we started to move quickly. "Slow down, big guy, easy on the oxygen. Okay, boys, on three: one, two, three." I floated upward, and the stars disappeared. Everything turned white. I realized I was in the back of a station wagon. My eyes fluttered in and out. I caught a glimpse of a man and woman wearing white clothes. Their hands darted over me time and time again. The door closed, and the crisp night air vanished.

Her blonde hair was neatly tucked under her cap. Her eyes met mine, and she smiled and mouthed, "You're going to be all right!" Deep down, I was unsure, but the thought of being all right was good enough for me when something sharp pierced my skin. I didn't know I could endure more pain, yet there it was. I felt an incredible calmness rush over me as my body went numb.

The cool night air awakened me once again. My eyes fluttered open. The stars returned, and the moon shined brightly in the night sky. A shiver ran down my spine. I guess that was a good sign. I could feel and sense my body. The pain throbbed in more places than I cared to count. But it was not as bad as before. A man wearing a blue mask hovered over me. I noticed a nurse or two huddled around as I was wheeled inside, where it was slightly warmer. *Why did they keep hospitals so cold? I wish I had been wearing my jacket. I was sure it was still in the car.*

"Where's April and Bobby?" I said from under my mask. No response. I shrugged. For a brief second, my body tingled, then soothed all over as the pain eased. My eyes rolled back a little, and I noticed the bag dangling from a pole beside me. *I liked that stuff.* I smiled under the plastic.

A light blinded me, and then I squinted again. The lights were evenly spaced out on the ceiling. They rolled past one after another as I looked up. I wondered where they were taking me. I must have counted over a dozen lights. I caught a glimpse of two large swinging doors. The cart stopped, and once again, they hoisted me up and swung me to yet another table.

People scurried about. *This was what Santa's workshop must look like*. Little people were darting here and there. Whatever they gave me in that drip bag made me feel funny and see things. *These were not elves, but why did they have pointy ears?* I giggled inside.

I tried to focus on the doctors and nurses, some in white and others in blue and green scrubs. I remembered when Larry at the shop cut his hand open, and I was tasked with driving him to the emergency room. The doctors and nurses all wore white. *I had to admit, I liked the added colors. Did the different colors mean anything? I have more power than you because I have dark blue scrubs, and you have light blue scrubs. Man, what did they put in that drip bag?*

The nurse hovered over me and started snipping away my shirt. *No, not the shirt. This was my favorite flannel shirt. It had just enough wear to feel perfect on the skin, and I liked the red, black, and gray checked pattern, too! Stop cutting my shirt*! I screamed on the inside. I didn't think my lips moved. The pants were next to be cut and removed—nothing special about my jeans. I owned several pairs of Lee jeans. I'd been wearing this brand since high school, maybe even longer. I couldn't be sure. They were the jeans that fit just right. You know the old saying, "If it ain't broke, don't fix it."

A giant size light blinded me; the beam seared my sight, and I had to close my eyes. That was great for the doctors and nurses but not so much for me. After all, they needed to see what they were working on. I tried to tilt my head to see, but I was strapped in one position. It finally occurred to me, *what if I couldn't walk? What if they had to cut off my leg or legs*? Fear riddled my body. I trembled and began to shake. *How would I take care of my family if I couldn't work?* I tried to move, bounced a little, and heard the doctor yell. "Morphine!"

TWO

Monday, October 16, 1961

My eyes bounced open. I blinked a few times as they adjusted to the light. The world wasn't red anymore. I quickly noticed something was obstructing my vision in my right eye. *Had I lost my sight?* I looked around, but I couldn't see anything. *Was I even awake?* Voices echoed in the distance. "Hello?" No response. *I must be dreaming. Did I even say anything? Was I the only one who heard my voice? What's happening?*

I felt that tingling sensation rushing over my body. *That stuff felt good—no pain for me.*

"How's he doing today?" a male voice said.

"He's stable. I just gave him another dose of meds." The nurse's voice was soft on my ears. Papers shuffled, and the clipboard echoed when someone placed it on the counter. Being a mechanic taught me a lot, like how to listen to sounds.

"Thanks. I'll check back in a little while," the male said.

"See you soon, Doc," she chuckled. *Was my nurse flirting with my doctor? Hey, hey, hey, none of that stuff. Focus and do your job!* I scolded her. I could hear her feet shuffle around. Moments later, the room fell silent.

I blinked. The room was dark, with just a soft light shining in the corner. A steady, peaceful, beeping tone bounced off the walls. My vision came into focus, and I tried to look around. I slowly regained my composure. The shade had been drawn, and from the looks of it, it was dark outside. *How long had I been here? I guess I was still in the hospital.* I looked to the other side of the room.

I gasped. "April!" I mouthed her name. The beeps grew quicker. Tears traced down my cheeks. She was alive, and I breathed a sigh of relief. Some of the guilt of the accident lifted from my shoulders. That was the best news I could have ever received. She was snuggled in the chair and half covered by a plaid blanket. I recognized her wavy blonde hair. She looked tired. *How long had she been here?* That didn't matter. She was healthy and alive. That was the main thing. The beeping noise slowed to a regular rhythm. *What about Bobby?* My eye darted back and forth. I didn't see Bobby. Panic set in. *What about Bobby?* I cried on the inside. *Where was my boy?* The beeping tone increased. "Where's Bobby?" The noise raced. The door flew open, and the nurse darted to my side. Quickly, she pulled out something, and within moments, my body tingled. I only wanted to know how Bobby was doing. I drifted to a land far away in my dreams.

"How's he doing today?" the doctor asked. He was picking up the chart and flipping through the pages.

"No change, Doc. So, how long do you think he'll be like this?" the nurse asked. Her voice was soothing. If I had to picture her in my mind, I would guess she was fresh out of college.

"The body will take as long as it needs to heal. Days, weeks, or even months. The good news is that he is healing and should fully recover with no side effects." He smiled.

"Did you hear that, Mr. Smithers? The doctor said you are healing fine and should return to normal soon. That is good news." The young nurse smiled. I watched as the doctor and the nurse left my room.

If I didn't know better, I'd say that young nurse was flirting with him. *That's not exactly what he said, dear. He said I should make a full recovery.* I watched her leave. Moments later, the door swung open again, and to my delight, it was April. *You're back,* I beamed from side to side. I cocked my eyebrow and scrunched my nose to get her attention. It worked. She waltzed up to me and sat on the edge of the bed. Her hand graced mine. April's fingers were cold. Thanks to the blanket, I managed to stay warm. "Hi, Bob," she whispered. I could hear her loud and clear. I moved my lips but realized there was a tube down my throat. *That explained why no one could hear me. Why didn't I think of that earlier?* I blinked several times so she knew I was listening to her. That was a first. *I was paying attention to what she had to say.* I could not take my eye off her smile. The doctor must have given her the good news. I couldn't wait to hold her in my arms again and kiss her. My eyes welled up. If I only had the strength to wipe the tears away...

She turned, picked something up, and faced me. Her arm stretched upward as I felt the soft touch of the hanky dab the tears away from my eye. *I wished I could see her with both eyes.* She was the best thing that ever happened to me. I remember the first time I saw her. *It was the summer of 1948. I was at the General Store with my third cousin, Tom. He was still training to take over his family's business. This car rolled up to the pump, and Tom went out to clean the windshield and gas up the car. I couldn't take my eyes off the 1948 Chrysler Town and Country. The car was pretty new. It was dark red with a woodgrain finish on the doors. The large whitewall tires looked sharp. I didn't know how anyone could afford a car like that. The starting price was $2,000.00.*

The passenger door opened, and this young woman, a goddess, stepped out. She was wearing a long, light-colored flower dress; I could see the tops of her white shoes. Her blonde hair was waving in the breeze. The burgundy hat made my heart melt. I didn't think anything was sexier than a woman wearing a hat. Her smile could brighten any room.

I panicked when I realized she was coming into the store. The bells rang over the door, and I froze. She asked me something, but I didn't remember what it was. I stared at her, and she asked me again. Oh, she wanted a cold Pepsi. What were the odds of that? I loved Pepsi, too. I escorted her to the cooler, opened the lid, grabbed her a cold one, and popped the top.

I gave her an awkward smile as I handed her the bottle. She had the prettiest blue eyes. I'd never been this nervous around another person before. I noticed the dimples on her cheeks as she blushed. "Hi, I'm April." The words rolled off her tongue. My heart skipped several beats.

"I'm Tom, I mean Bob," I chuckled, grinning with embarrassment.

"Are you sure?" April giggled.

"Yes, I'm Bob Smithers," I correctly introduced myself. She had the cutest giggle. She liked my last name, Smithers. I knew I wanted to marry this woman right away, and from how she giggled and blushed, I thought she was feeling the same about me. We exchanged names, and she told me where she lived. I only needed her father's permission to ask her out for dinner. A week later, I mustered up the nerve to ask him if I could see his daughter, and he clearly said "no" and slammed the door in my face.

I got back into my car, glanced up, and noticed April sitting in front of the upper window. She waved, and I was sure that would be the last time I saw her. Much to my surprise, April left a note with Tom at the store. She left word that she would be at the picture show on Saturday and requested that I meet her. I showed up promptly.

I glanced at her face as she leaned over the bed. I was pretty sure she had hit the dashboard or the windshield. Yet, she didn't have a scratch on her face. She must have been lucky. I wasn't as fortunate. I drifted in and out most of the day. Every time I opened my eyes, April sat in the chair in the corner of the room. She never left my side. *How did I get so lucky?*

I couldn't keep my eyes off April. I was sure she thought I was a crazed lunatic. She smiled every time she glanced in my direction. I couldn't remember what movie she told her father she would watch, but I convinced April to watch Key Largo. *It was a gangster movie. I only recalled a little about the film. We sat in the balcony section. I shared a bag of popcorn and a small Pepsi with April. She wasn't shy, and she knew what she wanted. And that was me. I was so nervous. Our fingers grazed once or twice in the pop-corn bag. Each time, she giggled, and I smiled. Before the night ended, she whispered, "Are you going to kiss me?" This was the first girl I kissed and still, to this day, the only woman I had ever kissed.*

I tilted my head to the side and noticed it was dark out-side. Different nurses came and went. The only person who stayed by my side was April. *How could I be so careless with my driving?*

If I only knew about Bobby. I'm sure he was okay, or April would have mentioned it by now. I didn't know how long or how many days I have been in the hospital. I was only guessing that it was two or three weeks.

I knew I was starting to feel better. I could sense it. Then my eyes fluttered open. Much to my surprise, the room was empty. My eyes adjusted, and my vision was clearer today. The doctor must have removed the eye patch. I could see with both eyes.

I heard two men talking in the hallway. They appeared to be standing in front of my door. I recognized one of the voices. It was my cousin, Tom. *He must have hired someone to watch the store for him or flat-out closed the store so he could visit me.* I smiled on the inside. *Tom was a good man.*

The other voice must be the doctor. The words muffled through the door, and I could only make out a few of them— my name and something about April. *What about April? Where was she? Maybe April was covering for Tom at the store. That would make sense. I hope it wasn't because she and Bobby needed money. The last thing I wanted was for April to ask her father for money. We had been together for over ten years, and I hadn't borrowed a dime from the man.*

I knew he never wanted me to marry his daughter. I was just some mechanic at the local garage. I couldn't provide for his daughter, not the way he or some rich guy could. But it wasn't his choice. It was April's, and she loved me.

April and her mother were close. Maria, April's mother, was okay with us being together. She invited us over for all the holidays and, occasionally, just for dinner. Bobby also adored his grandmother. The three would go shopping twice a month, and Bobby would always come home with a new toy. It also explained where April got some of her clothes.

April was proud of me, and that was all that mattered. I was also proud that I had never taken a dime from them. I had a good job and provided for my family. None of us were going hungry. When the time was right, we purchased the house of our dreams on the river. I had added a room for Bobby when he was born. It helped to be handy. I also added the garage when I bought the new car. We have almost five acres of land and plenty of room to expand.

The door pushed open, and the young nurse waltzed in. She began checking the equipment as she jotted notes on her clipboard. I felt her fingers on my arm and throat. She moseyed over to the other side of the bed, pulled out the pan, and replaced it with a clean one. *It's the same routine day after day. That begged the question, how long had I been here?*

I heard the door hinge squeak again. "Hello, doctor," the nurse said.

"Hello," he paused, taking the chart from the nurse. He flipped through the pages rather quickly. "Your vitals look good. Everything is falling into place." He smiled. "So, how are you feeling, Bob?"

The hinges squeaked again. "Hi Doc. Hello, nurse Betty."

"Call me Michael." The doctor hung the chart at the foot of the bed.

"Any updates for me today?" Tom asked.

"No, he's still in a coma," the doc replied.

"Dang, Bob's gonna flip his lid when he wakes."

"He could wake up any day now," the doctor added. "It's the one part of my job that I don't like. Telling someone his wife and son didn't survive."

"What?" I choked out. It was hard to talk with this tube stuck in my throat. My eyes fluttered and slowly opened. Tom came into view. His eyes bulged, and his mouth hung open. Startled, the young nurse jumped back like she had seen a ghost. Doctor Michael spun on his heels to get a look at me.

"Well, look who is waking up!"

"April," I managed to spit out. "Where's April?" my voice slurred. A tear traced down the side of my face. "Bobby?" The floodgates opened, and I balled my hands at my side and started to bang the mattress.

Doctor Michael rushed to my side and restrained my arms. "Morphine," he blurted out.

A warm, tingly feeling rushed over me. I stared at the ceiling, trying to understand what I had just heard. *Were Bobby and April gone?*

THREE

Sunday, November 12, 1961

My eyes flickered as the ceiling came into view. My throat was sore. "Thirsty," I struggled to say. Tom woke and appeared stunned as he grabbed the glass of water and bolted to my side in a flash. He placed the straw to my lips.

"Drink slow," he whispered.

I pursed my lips together and took a sip. Ah, the cool water soothed my throat. I paused to take a breath, then took another sip. I gazed at Tom. He looked rough, tired, and obviously like a man who hadn't shaved for days. His eyes told a story. One filled with pain and sorrow. I could tell something troubled Tom. I watched as he pushed a button along the side of the bed.

The door swung open, and Dr. Michael entered, along with a nurse. She stood in the far corner and looked nervous. My eyes darted back and forth, wanting to know what was wrong. I pushed my lips together. "Hi" was all I could muster.

"Hello, Bob." The doctor nodded. "Do you know where you are?"

"Yes, hospital," I grunted.

"That's good. I'm glad to see you are awake. Let me check your vitals and see how you are doing." The doctor stepped forward, placed his fingers on my hand, and worked his way up my arm and down the other side. His hands felt cold on my neck and chest. The nurse stepped forward, pulling the sheets back as he worked toward my feet. I caught a glimpse of my broken right leg. My right hip was also in pain, and my left arm was sore.

"Well, Bob, things are healing pretty good. We can get you out of here in another week or two.

"How long?" My throat was dry, and I pointed to the water.

"Like I just mentioned, another week or two."

"No, how long…" I paused. "Been here?" The doctor nodded, so I knew he knew what I was asking.

"If my math is correct, about twenty-seven days."

"April? Bobby?" I could sense something was terribly wrong. Tom stepped back, and the young nurse turned to the table and pretended to take notes. "Well?" My speech improved with every water sip.

"Mr. Smithers…" The doctor took a deep breath. "Your wife April and son Bobby didn't survive the crash." The doctor just stared at me. I guess he was waiting for my reaction.

I blinked a few times as the tears welled in my eyes. Tom moved to my side and laid his hand on mine. I could tell he was hurting, too. I gazed at the doctor, and he nodded to the nurse. "We'll give you some time. I'll be back in a little while." I watched the door close behind them, and the floodgates opened.

April and Bobby had been stripped from my life forever. I had never felt this kind of pain. *But how could that be? I spoke to April yesterday.* It took several minutes before I could regain my composure. I wiped my eyes and looked up at Tom; our eyes locked. "Why?"

"I wish I had an answer." Tom frowned. "They say when our time is up, it's up."

"Don't give me that crap!" I yelled as best I could. "You and I both know this is my fault."

"Don't be hard on yourself. I'm sure you did everything possible to avoid the other car." Tom tried to cheer me up, but nothing he could say would change my mind. We sat in silence for several moments until I calmed down. Tom leaned forward. "What do you remember about that night?"

I was puzzled by Tom's question. I flashed back to that night. "We were at the bowling alley. It was Bobby's tenth birthday party," I spoke softly. I could see his smile and hear his laughter as I recounted the night. "He and his friends were bowling. April sat with the other mothers, chatting, oblivious to their surroundings. A couple of the dads and I watched the boys and offered bowling tips when possible. Bobby rolled a 96, and I hoped he would roll his first 100. We served cake and had ice cream." *That would be the last great memory of Bobby and April that I ever had.*

I made eye contact with Tom and frowned. This next part would be painful. "After the party, we loaded the presents into the car and headed for the house. Bobby couldn't stop talking about his buddies and how well he bowled." I spoke slowly, remembering how excited he was. "We were less than a mile from the house. Lights blinded me as I crested the top of the hill. That's when things get blurry." I shook my head in frustration. "That's all I remember."

"I wasn't sure what you remembered. Maybe more will come back to you in time," Tom said.

"What have you heard from the police or the doctor? Oh gosh…" My stomach turned, and I panicked. "What about the other driver? Tell me it wasn't a family."

Tom opened, then closed his mouth. He frowned slightly. "There was only one person in the other car." He paused, thinking that would satisfy me, but it didn't. I needed more.

"The other driver, were they hurt or, worse, killed?" I tried to sit up.

"Bob, you need to relax." Tom leaned me back as he fluffed the pillow.

"I need to know," I begged.

"There was only one person in the car. It was a young man about sixteen. Just like you, he's going to be all right." Tom frowned.

I breathed a sigh of relief. "Do I know the guy or his family?"

"I don't think so. The kid lived on the other side of the mountain. A small town called Sugar Valley," Tom explained.

"What aren't you telling me?" I'd known Tom all my life. We were cousins. His facial expression told me he was hiding something. I was determined to find out what it was.

"I've told you everything I know." Tom turned his back to me and looked out the window.

"Liar," I spat out. I didn't mean it to sound so harsh, but the words were already out of my mouth.

"Calm down, all right? I'll tell you everything I know to this point." Tom turned and laid his hand on the chair, scooting it toward the side of my bed. I studied him as he sat. Our eyes locked, and he bowed his head.

"Tom, look me in the eyes and tell me everything," I pleaded and frowned as my eyes widened.

"All right." He nodded, falling to my plea. "The other driver was sixteen. He had only been driving a few months. He walked away with a broken arm and a few minor scratches."

"And?" I barked.

"There's nothing more to tell."

"Bullshit. I know you're hiding something. Now spill the beans before I give you a knuckle sandwich." My patience was wearing thin. Tom smiled, knowing I was in no condition to fight him. I could tell Tom didn't want to share something with me, and I was determined to find out what it was, even if it killed me. "I would rather hear it from you, Tom, than someone else. So please tell me everything. I'm not a child."

"The driver was sixteen."

"You said that once!" I screamed. "Damn it, man, tell me everything. I know you have friends at the station. After all, they shop at your store. So, stop beating around the bush and tell me. Now!" I yelled.

The door creaked open. Nurse Betty strolled to the side of my bed. "Is everything all right, Bob?"

"Everything's fine," Tom explained. "Can you give me a few more minutes? Please."

"It's getting late." Nurse Betty paused, giving me a little nod. "Just a few more minutes."

I smiled back and watched the door close behind her. "You were saying?"

Tom took a deep breath. "The boy's name was James Jones, and his nickname was J.J. He had only been driving for a few months. The police report stated that he had been drinking." Tom stopped, giving me a second to process this.

"What?" I hollered. "Are you telling me some kid was drunk—a kid, and he was drinking? He killed April and Bobby? That's… that's ridiculous. Who would let their kid drink and drive? Is he in jail?" My head spun, and I was angry—so many questions needed to be answered.

"Relax and take a deep breath." Tom placed his hand on mine. "No, he's not in jail. The kid pleaded guilty to underage drinking," Tom said and looked away.

"How on earth could the judge just let him off?"

"I think his family comes from money."

"Of course, it's always about the money." I shook my head, disgusted. "But that doesn't excuse the kid from what he did." I teared up.

"You're right," Tom said, his eyes showing concern for my well-being. *That had to be hard on him, giving me the bad news.* I softened a little. There was so much I wanted to say, scream, or yell. But, I needed to focus on getting out of the hospital, finding out all I could about this J.J. boy, and making sure he rots in jail.

"Tom," I said calmly. "I need to be alone. "

"I understand, Bob." He stood and walked toward the door. Tom turned. "I'm sorry."

"Me too." I gritted my teeth, trying to hide my pain and anger.

"I'll see you tomorrow. Try to get some sleep," Tom added and closed the door.

FOUR

Friday, December 1, 1961

I'm still mad at myself for not avoiding the other car that fateful night. I was even more upset that the other driver was only sixteen. Why was he allowed to drive at night at such a young age? Not to mention he had been drinking, which still makes my blood boil. Tom told me the judge said he was a minor and had pleaded guilty to underage drinking. How could the system let him off? Did the lives of my wife and son mean nothing? They meant the world to me. Am I bitter? Yes. But there wasn't much I could do from inside the hospital.

Today represented freedom. Seven weeks had passed since the accident. I was moving around pretty well. The doctor said I would use a cane for a bit longer but should return to normal in a month or two. I hoped to get out today but dreaded going to an empty home. That explains why I was a mixed bag of emotions. Nurse Betty was in to see me and helped me get my stuff together, and Doctor Michael had signed the paperwork and said his goodbyes. Now, I just had to sit and wait for Tom. I paced back and forth from the window, where I had a great view of the parking lot, to the door, where I gazed down the corridor.

Patience was never my strong suit. What was taking Tom so long? Fridays are paydays, so he was probably busy pumping gas and selling milk and bread at the store. But what about me? Couldn't he take a few minutes for me? After all, I hadn't been home in forever. As I returned to the window, the door creaked open. "It's about time," I barked. Nurse Betty strolled in, pushing a wheelchair. "What is that?" I snapped.

"I have to push you out. It's policy. But if you keep snapping at me, I might push you down the stairs." Betty giggled and smiled. Her blue eyes could melt any heart. Even an angry one like mine.

"I'm sorry." I paused. "I would like to go home." I softened. She was a sweet lady and didn't deserve my smart-ass remarks. I'm thankful she had a great personality.

"I understand, Mr. Smithers." She motioned me to sit in the chair.

Betty handed me a paper bag with my belongings inside. The bag was smaller than I would have imagined, partly because they ruined my good jeans and my favorite flannel shirt. I turned around and eased my behind into the wheelchair. Betty folded the foot pegs out for me to place my feet on. We gently lunged forward, pausing at the door for one last glance at my room. We rolled down the hallway past the nurse's station, where several ladies waved and wished me luck. I could sense they were whispering and talking behind my back. *I didn't need anyone's pity.*

The elevator door slid open. Betty wasted no time getting us inside and pushing the button. I wondered if she was happy to see me leave. *Had I been that much of a pain?* The elevator car descended slowly and then bounced to a stop. The door slid open, and much to my surprise, Doctor Michael and several of his staff members greeted me one last time. My boss stood next to him. He whispered, "Take all the time you need, and when you're ready, come back to work." A few of my co-workers cheered for me. Several of the guys I bowled with waited to see me off. My eyes watered. I had forgotten how much these people meant to me. I would have never imagined.

I rolled past, shaking everyone's hand and hiding my emotions. It was a losing battle. Standing at the end of the line was Tom. If I didn't know better, I would have thought he'd planned this. I forced a smile.

I froze when I spotted April. My body shivered. *How could she be alive? Why would they lie to me?* She was looking directly at me. I smirked and looked around. *Was this a cruel joke?* She smiled back. Tom stepped forward, passing through her, and she evaporated before my eyes. I gripped the armrest on the wheelchair, and my eyes bulged. I trembled, and my heart rate soared to new heights. I looked at Tom and then back to where April had stood.

"Are you all right?" Tom asked.

I knew I had just seen April. She was standing right in front of me. I must have wanted to see April so badly that my mind played tricks on me. Was I losing my mind?

If I said something, Tom would think I was crazy, and I didn't want to go to the crazy ward. The grief counselor had been stopping for an hour a day, three times a week. I was not too fond of those sessions. "I'm fine, just happy to see everyone." I hid my pain.

I looked around the crowd. I won't forget this. These folks were amazing, true friends. I said my final goodbyes. With Tom's help, I stood and eased my way into the passenger seat. Everything I tried to do was difficult. I looked one last time at the crowd and waved as the engine roared to life. "Thank you for setting this up. You're a great guy."

"You're welcome," Tom said.

I sat in silence as we drove through downtown Lock Haven. I stared out the window and watched businesses roll by. I knew them all too well. We passed the car dealership where I worked and then rode over the Bald Eagle River bridge. Red silos dotted the countryside, and that helped to put my mind at ease. Next, Tom and I cruised through the small town of Mill Hall and quickly made our way to Lizardville Road, where we turned left, past Tom's General Store and Gas. The red sign on the door read "Closed." Another mile further up the river, Tom slowed, making the sharp left-hand turn into my gravel driveway. The crushed rock roared to life as we drove between the heavy brush that hid my house from the world.

The freshly cut lawn stretched to the tree line where my property met the woods. My tiny cottage-style home sat nestled along the banks of Big Fishing Creek. The towering bluffs on the far side of the river always amazed me. The car rolled to a stop, and Tom turned off the engine. I gazed out the windshield as Tom did the same.

"Are you okay?" Tom broke the silence.

"I'm fine," I lied. "Thank you for all your help today," I said, pulling the latch and shoving the door open. I stepped out, holding the small paper sack in my left arm and the cane in my right. The driver's door swung open. I quickly turned. "Please, I need to do this myself." Tom looked in my direction, nodded, and shut his door. I took a few steps. Before he left, Tom backed the car around and told me to call if I needed anything.

I stopped at the base of the stairs. I counted each step until I reached five. I took a long breath, pulled the keys from my pocket, and unlocked the door. I tapped the door open with my cane. At first glance, everything looked the same. I closed the door behind me. The silence was something I would have to get used to.

I had never lived alone. My first apartment I shared with Tom. We both worked all the time and were mainly home in the evenings. Then I met April, and she stayed with Tom and me until we bought this place. Our house. Now, my house again. My lonely castle. *How would I survive without April and Bobby?*

The house plants in the window were brown and dried out. A musty odor loomed in the air. I strolled past and made my way to the kitchen. The dishes were still sitting on the drying rack. *I'll put them away later.* I flipped the latch and pushed the window upward. I walked to the other side of the living room and pushed up the large window behind the couch.

A nice, cold breeze blew past. How I wish it were summer. I couldn't leave the windows open too long, or I would freeze to death. That would be a good idea. *What did I have to live for anyway?*

The tapping sound of the cane reminded me of how quiet things were as I made my way to my bedroom. I paused in front of Bobby's room, his toys still scattered on the floor. I could hear his laughter. I walked to my bedroom with many reminders of April and Bobby inside. The room began to spin, and I knelt over, placing a hand at the foot of the bed. I needed clarification. I needed to lie down. I crawled onto the bed. It had been so long since I laid on a comfortable mattress. I closed my eyes, hoping the dizziness would fade.

I woke to the sound of Bobby playing in his room. I could hear dice rolling and Bobby counting as he moved the pieces to the game. I'm sure he was playing *Sorry*. That was his favorite since his grandparents gave him the game last year at Christmas. "Dinner's ready," April hollered. "Come on, boys. It's time to eat."

Hunger set in. Forgetting my cane, I rolled out of bed and walked to the door. I limped down the hallway—Past Bobby's room, where I glanced to see *Sorry* laid out on the floor. *I guess I was right. After dinner, we could all play as a family.* I inhaled, and the smell of the chicken overwhelmed me. *I loved the way April prepared her meals.* My tummy growled and turned over. I went down the hallway, hearing April and Bobby laughing. I rounded the corner to an empty room. I froze. I heard Bobby and April. I didn't imagine it. I could smell the chicken. It was real.

Tears filled my eyes. I tugged at my hair and gritted my teeth. They were here. I know they were here. I crouched, sat on the floor, and rocked back and forth. *Was I losing my mind? I just heard them!* "Bobby, April," I cried out. I sat on the floor until my eyes ran out of tears. I had almost convinced myself that what I heard and smelled was real. *But it couldn't be.*

I was still hungry. I carefully got myself back to my feet, walked to the refrigerator, and pulled the handle. I saw a half gallon of unopened milk, lunch meat, and a small pot of stew with a note on top that read, "Welcome home." Tom had thought of everything. I noticed a loaf of bread on the counter. My heart warmed. I picked up the phone, placed my finger in the number seven hole, and spun the rotary dial. I watched as each number spun back to the beginning. The phone began to ring. I waited patiently until Tom finally answered.

FIVE

I rolled to the edge of my bed. I swung my legs over the side and felt the warmth of the slippers on my bare feet. I stood, stretched, and gazed out the window. I'd forgotten how pretty a layer of freshly fallen snow could look. It was a good reason not to leave the house.

It's hard to get excited when everything I loved and lived for has been ripped away. Tom kept hounding me about putting up a Christmas tree. After all, it was only a few weeks away. *Why bother?* It was only me.

It's been almost two months since that dreadful night. *How was I supposed to celebrate?* Mentally, I was not ready. I didn't want anyone's pity, either. Tom was the only one who cared. I valued that.

Now that I think of it, April's mother and father had only checked on me once in the hospital. I'm sure that was to see if I would live or die. I know how her father felt about me, and with April and Bobby out of the picture, I was optimistic that I would never hear or see from either of them again. How quickly things change.

The dice rolling on the wooden floor caught my attention. *It was too early for Bobby to be up. That kid loved to play his board games.* I smiled and proceeded down the hallway. My leg was healing well, and the pain was almost gone. I paused to look in Bobby's room. I noticed snake eyes on the dice. *He would get another turn.* A shiver ran down my spine, and I returned to reality. My eyes darted back and forth. I trembled, and my mouth hung open. I cleaned up the room a week ago. I stepped in. How did the *Sorry* game end up in the middle of the floor? I stepped lightly toward the closet and slowly opened the door. There was nothing inside except Bobby's clothes and toys neatly stacked the way I had placed them. I felt something was off. I grabbed his wooden baseball bat. I felt the need to defend myself. I turned and set one foot before the other, slowly stepping over the *Sorry* game. I exited the door and went into the hallway. My heart was racing. *Who was in the house? Who would play such a mean trick?* I cautiously proceeded to the end of the hallway and peeked around the corner. The kitchen was deserted. I gazed at the windows. They were closed and appeared to be locked. I went to the vacant living room and quickly dashed to the front door. I stepped back when I realized it was unlocked.

I always remember to lock the door. My mind scurried to last night. *I was watching the television. I drifted off, woke up, and stumbled to bed. I don't remember locking the door. How could I forget?* I nervously placed my hand on the knob and slowly tugged it open.

An undisturbed layer of snow covered the porch. I breathed a sigh of relief. No footprints. I jiggled the handle on the glass storm door. It was locked. My detective sense kicked in. No one came in this way. I closed the front door and locked it. I even slid the chain lock on the top just to be safe. What would anyone want with me? I didn't own anything of value, and I barely had any extra money. I went to the mud room to check the final two doors. I twisted the handle to the basement. It was locked. I always kept it shut. It was dark, and Bobby had been just a few inches shy of reaching the string to turn on the light. The last thing I needed was for him to fall down the stairs.

My hand twitched as I moved closer to the back door. I grabbed the final doorknob. It was locked. A calm rushed over me. The house was secure. But that didn't explain how the game ended up on the floor. I must be losing my mind. I took a deep breath and went to the kitchen to make coffee. The Lord knows I could use a cup about now.

I laid the baseball bat on the table and watched the water percolate and bubble. The dark brown juice dripped into the pot below. I pulled my mug from the sink and poured myself a cup. I added two spoonful's of sugar and a dash of milk. I slowly raised it to my lips and felt relief flush over me. I sat at the table, nursing the cup of java to the last drop. I needed my newspaper, which meant I needed to go outside and brave the cold weather as I walked to the end of the driveway. The news would have to wait.

I poured myself another cup of coffee, stood, and went to Bobby's room. I crossed the entryway and froze. I felt a lump in my throat. Then I heard my coffee mug shatter on the floor. My eyes welled up. *The game was gone.* It was here a few minutes ago. No one was here except me. I stepped back, and a tear traced down my cheek. *I'm losing my mind. I know what I saw. The game was right here.* I stepped back into the hallway. I twisted my fingers in my hair and tugged, pulled, and let out a scream. I placed my back on the wall and lowered myself to the floor. I repeatedly yelled Bobby's name until my throat hurt.

I woke, lying on my side in the hallway. I sat up and turned the corner, seeing only my broken coffee mug and a sizeable brown stain on the wooden floor. I trembled briefly before entering the closet to get the broom and dustpan. I could not leave broken glass lying around, not in Bobby's room.

SIX

Monday, December 25, 1961

Unlike Christmas the past few years, I woke to silence and the smell of an abandoned home. April would have been in the kitchen cooking our Christmas dinner. The scent of turkey would have filled the house. Bobby would have been bouncing around, waiting to get into his presents.

April always let him open one gift to keep him happy, allowing me time to sleep in. It was one of the only days of the year I could get extra sleep. I sat up, glanced at the clock, and was stunned to see it was after ten. Tom said he would come over for dinner, which meant lunch.

I walked to the kitchen and put on a pot of coffee. I then strolled to the bathroom to shower and put on some clean clothes since I often found myself sleeping in the clothes from the day before. I returned to the kitchen, poured a cup of coffee, and took a long drink. Then I opened my mouth and fanned it with my hand *like that would help my burnt tongue*. I moved to the freezer and grabbed two turkey Swanson TV dinners. I laid them on the counter to thaw. I was sure Tom would understand.

I gave the house a quick look over. I didn't have time to run the vacuum. That would have to wait. I grabbed the stack of old newspapers and a few paper plates from the coffee table and stuffed them into the trash. I picked up several coffee mugs and turned on the faucet. I gazed out the window and watched the steam rise from the creek. It was barely twenty degrees outside. The water flowed slowly, and the trees were lightly covered with snow. How picturesque.

I ran my finger under the faucet and quickly jerked back. Pain shot through me because the water was hot. *Dang, that was stupid.* I turned the cold water to equal the hot water and added soap to my sponge. I stacked the mugs, one by one, in the drainer on the side of the sink. I watched a pair of squirrels playing tag in the trees. *The cold weather didn't bother them.* I picked up the towel to dry the mugs. I started to wipe the first coffee mug and heard it shatter as it slipped from my fingers. I was frozen at the moment. My head jerked forward, and I gazed out the window again.

Bobby darted past the window, and I pulled back. I rushed to the front door. I was unlatching the lock and pulling the chain back. I flung the door open and darted outside. "Bobby," I mumbled. *He was not going to hear me like that.* "Bobby!" I yelled at the top of my lungs and quickly stepped off the porch and sprinted to the backyard facing the creek. He wasn't here. I looked in both directions and raced to the side yard, then out front and back to the stream. *I had just seen Bobby. I know I did. I did not imagine him! Or did I?* I wanted to start my Christmas differently.

I stood in silence; a shiver ran down my spine. I don't know how long I had been standing there. I trembled from top to bottom. My head snapped toward the kitchen window when I heard April's voice singing. One second, she was standing there. The next, she was gone, vanished right before my eyes. I turned to face the creek. *I must be seeing things, losing my mind.* That's the only explanation. I had finished taking the medicine the doctor prescribed a month ago and had no alcohol in months. That left only one option. I was going crazy.

"You're going to catch cold standing out here in your bare feet."

"Jeepers, Creepers!" I screamed and jumped a foot in the air. My head spun so fast it hurt. "What the heck, Tom?" My heart pounded in my chest. I paused, placing my hands on my knees to catch my breath. After a brief minute, I straightened up. "That's a good way to get a knuckle sandwich," I gritted.

"What are you doing out here?"

"I thought I saw something."

"Deer, bear, what?" Tom's eyes drilled into me.

"Bobby," I stuttered.

Tom stepped forward and draped his arm over my shoulders. "Come on, Bob, let's get you inside, and you can tell me all about it."

The warmth of the house felt good. Tom ushered me to the couch and helped me ease into the soft cushions. I watched Tom shuffle around the kitchen. First, he placed a hot cup of coffee before me. "Give it a minute, or you will burn your mouth."

I nodded. *I'd been there and done that,* I thought. I watched as Tom disappeared down the hallway. I was trying to figure out what I should tell Tom, if anything. Or how to explain what I had been hearing and seeing. *Would he even understand or believe me? Or would he call the guys with the white coats and have them lock me up because I'd gone over the edge?*

Tom returned with a large tin wash tub half full of water. I watched the steam rise. "Lower your feet in here slowly," he said as he placed the container before me. "Easy, now." Tom rolled up my pant legs to prevent them from getting soaked. It was kind of late for that, but why make matters worse? Tom helped me guide my feet in. I thought it would hurt or burn.

"How does it feel?"

"I don't feel anything." I apologized.

"How long were you outside? You know you could get frostbite and lose your toes or even a foot or two," Tom scolded.

I remember one time when I was young and got into a snowball fight at school with a few other boys. I removed my mittens to pack a tighter snowball. I knew that it was easier to throw them, and they hurt more when they hit if they were packed tightly. Then I lost one of my mittens and almost lost one of my fingers from frostbite. The teacher scolded me, and I got into more trouble when I got home. "I'm sorry," I felt like a little child again.

"Let me know if you feel anything at all." His eyes and voice were concerned.

I nodded. Tom walked to the TV and turned it on before heading into the kitchen. I heard him chuckle. "We both had the same idea." He turned, holding my two Swanson turkey TV dinners. "I brought two, and you had two." He laughed.

"Hey, how about I cook all four, and we have two each. Let's pig out like old times." He turned the dial on the oven.

I turned my attention to the television. "'Babes in Toyland,' starring Shirley Temple, will air tonight at 7:00 p.m. on NBC, followed by *The Dinah Shore Show* at 9:00 p.m. Now, back to our movie," the commenter said. It was *The Pied Piper*. I had seen this one before. It had been around for several years. I guess the overcast skies made my picture a little fuzzy today. "Hey Tom, I wonder if you could go out and turn the antenna to the right a little."

Tom turned and looked at the black-and-white picture. "It's fine. Besides, we're going to eat anyway, and it will give us a chance to catch up." He turned his attention back to the kitchen.

Terrific. Tom wanted to talk. I would rather watch this old rerun. Then, I felt a tingle in my right foot. A few moments later, I felt it on my left foot. "Tom, my feet are tingling."

Tom turned and smiled. "That's good news. It looks like you will not lose your feet after all."

"What do you mean?" I said in a sarcastic tone.

"It will only be a matter of time if you keep going outside in your bare feet before you lose one." Tom smiled. "Then I would have to take care of you or put you in the old people's home." Tom laughed as he tossed me a towel. "Dry your feet and put the socks and slippers on, and come over here and sit down. Dinner is almost ready."

"You're starting to sound like my wife." I pushed back as I slid one sock on my right foot, then the other on my left.

The oven timer dinged. I stood and slipped on my slippers as I walked to the table. Tom placed one of the TV dinners and a large glass of milk before me. *That's right.*

I love milk. Tom sat across from me, and we plowed into our meals.

I felt terrible in a way. It was my turn to cook and prepare everything, and once again, it was Tom to my rescue. We finished the first meal and decided to go for the second. My stomach ached, and I felt uncomfortable. It felt like a real Christmas, well, almost. I did help Tom clean up before taking my spot on the couch. A few moments later, Tom sat on the left side of me.

"So, tell me, Bob, what's this about seeing Bobby this morning?" His voice was riddled with empathy.

"Well," I paused and took a deep breath. *Here goes nothing*. "I was standing over the sink washing coffee cups while watching the squirrels playing in the trees. Something… someone… okay, Bobby ran past in his black-and-red snowsuit." I glanced at Tom. He never said a word, but by his look, he seemed interested in what I was saying, so I continued. "For a second, I thought I was seeing things or losing my mind. I mean, I may be nuts for all I know. But it was Bobby, clear as when he was alive," I stuttered. *That was hard to say out loud*. "I know what you must be thinking."

"I believe you, Bob, and I understand," Tom said with a half-smile.

I was stunned and speechless. *Tom said he believed me*. I continued. "When I spotted Bobby, I ran outside to see if he was there. I didn't think about anything, no shoes or coat. I only wanted to see Bobby and hold him in my arms. I love him, and I, I…" *I couldn't finish my sentence*. My eyes went blurry, and my cheeks were soaked as the tears flowed.

"It will be all right. I promise." Tom slid closer. I felt the warm embrace as he pulled me close to his body.

It was time to get this off my chest. "When I was in the hospital for eight weeks, I spoke with April every day. Afternoons, evenings, and even the early morning hours. She was always by my side." I sobbed. Confessing everything to Tom felt like a weight being lifted from my shoulders. I felt calm and relaxed, but I would never be able to erase my guilt and pain.

"Let it all out. Let it all out." Tom embraced me.

We sat and talked for hours. Our Christmas dinner together was excellent. Tom felt like the only family member I had left. I knew inside that April's parents would never stop by, but they could have at least sent a card. After all, I remembered to send them a card.

SEVEN

Friday, March 30, 1962

My life was getting somewhat back to normal. I worked at the garage five days a week, and everyone treated me nicely. So many times, I felt they were walking on eggshells around me, trying not to say something that would upset me or make me cry. It was nice getting back into a routine and being around people. I'd learned to appreciate everything I have in this world and the people around me.

The owners at the dealership and several of the bosses and sales guys all pitched in to help with the medical bills. It was nice and unexpected. But it helped me out of a jam. I don't know how I would have ever been able to pay off that debt. The sales manager even let me drive one of the company's loaner cars. I'm still driving it today. It's a new 1961 Plymouth Belvedere. It has a 318 horsepower Slant Six engine. Not that I wanted a car with a lot of power. The six-cylinder helped me save on gas. I couldn't believe I was paying thirty-two cents a gallon for gas. If the price increased, I may have to start riding a bike to work. I'd even thought about doing that in the summer.

But with all the good things that were happening, I still had one issue. I always cringed when I saw one of the local teenage boys stop by to look at the cars. They shouldn't allow them to drive. I didn't know if I could forgive the boy who took my family away. *Even when I saw them at Tom's store, my blood boiled. They hurt me. Now I wanted to hurt them, yes, all of them. I knew that's not normal. But what was normal?*

I looked at the clock on the wall, ten minutes after five. I wrapped things up and cleaned my workstation. The weekend was here—the start of another long, lonely weekend. I grabbed my lunch pail and walked to the time clock. I picked up my card and heard the click as it punched me out.

I unlocked my car and climbed in, rolling the window down to enjoy the spring weather. I inserted the key and twisted it. The engine roared. I loved the sound of this car. I cherished this baby like it was my own. *Maybe I should buy it.* I drove through town, the breeze slapping me in the face, and down a few windy roads. Then I turned onto Lizardville Road. I glanced at my gas gauge. I still had over half a tank. *Oh well. I'll stop by, top off the tank, and see what cousin Tom is up to.*

The small metal railing on the bridge came into view. I slowed as I crossed Big Fishing Creek and turned left into Tom's General Store and Gas. I heard the bells clang as I rolled over the black rubber hose beside the gas pump.

The front door sprung open, and out strolled Tom. "Hey Bob, are you here to top off the tank?"

"I sure am." I smiled and watched as Tom went to the rear of the car and knelt. I could hear the squeak of the license plate as he pulled it downward. *It was funny how you could hear the little things in life when you took the time to listen. I was getting good at that now that I lived alone.* He inserted the gas nozzle, and the numbers on the pump began to flip.

"Can I check your oil?"

"No thanks, you checked it last week," I hollered.

Tom grabbed the squeegee, plopped it on my windshield, and pushed it back and forth to clean the bugs off. It was customary even when the windshield was almost spotless. Tom called it excellent customer service. The pump clicked off, and Tom went to the back to round off the amount to an even number. After he hung up the pump handle, he turned to me. "That will be two dollars and fifty cents."

"What, no family discount?"

"We go through this every week, Bob, but today, I'll let you have it for five bucks." Tom chuckled.

"I'm sorry, who are you? I'll take the normal customer rate if you don't mind." I pulled three dollars from my wallet and handed them to Tom. "I'm shocked. I didn't think it would take eight gallons." I frowned.

"Any big plans this weekend?" Tom handed me fifty cents.

"Not really. I will mow the yard this weekend and start working on my garden," I said.

"Well, maybe I'll bring a six-pack of beer over Sunday, and we can watch the Phillies play baseball?" Tom said.

"Oh, you know I don't drink anymore, but you are welcome to come over and bring some beer for yourself," I replied. Tom stepped back and gave me an odd look.

"I'll see you around one on Sunday," Tom said.

"That sounds like a plan." I smiled, turned the key, and slowly pulled away. As I rolled down the road, I noticed two young boys walking along the side of the street. They were carrying a small tackle box and fishing poles. *They had to be up to no good.* I glanced at my rearview mirror and watched them fade as I rounded the next corner. They never looked back in my direction. My blood boiled, and I knew I was right. *They had to be up to something—no good, rotten kids. They would be out on the street driving cars and killing families in a few years.*

I growled and slowed as I approached my driveway. I turned on my left turn signal. I don't know why, though. I rarely noticed any other cars on this stretch of roadway. The gravel crunched under my tires, and I pulled alongside the house and stopped. I rolled up my window, stepped out, and locked the door behind me. I didn't trust those boys; the last thing I needed was them messing with my baby.

I walked up to the door with my lunch pail in hand. I pulled the keys out, shoved them into the lock, and twisted. With my hip, I bumped the door open. I froze, losing my grip on the lunch pail as it tumbled to the floor. I blinked a few times, swallowed hard, and stepped over the lunch bucket. I rubbed my chin, my eyes fixed on the coffee table. That was impossible; I had packed that away. A tear traced down the side of my cheek. My mind whirled, and my heart filled with rage. I dashed to my car, not even closing the front door behind me.

Those boys were going to pay for this. *No one messes with me and gets away with it.* I sped out of the drive, gravel flying up behind me. I quickly glanced to the left to ensure there was no traffic and burned rubber. I shot down the road looking for those so-called fishermen. I raced back to Tom's store. I turned around in his parking lot and slowly backtracked to my house. I was cautious this time. I didn't want to miss them. I peeked over the embankment to the water's edge and followed the creek upstream. Lizardville Road followed the stream for the next mile. I slowed and gazed through the trees. I pushed the brakes and came to an abrupt stop, then put the car in reverse and backed up a little. *No, it was just a deer.* I continued to drive, making sure not to miss them. *Those boys must have been good at hiding. Or possibly they hightailed it up the mountainside or took one of the trails to their home.*

I arrived back at my driveway as disappointment set in. I don't know how I lost those boys. I wish I had gotten a better look at their faces when I drove past them the first time. I parked the car and looked at my mess, gravel thrown everywhere. I guess that was something else I needed to add to my spring-cleaning list. *No, no, I need a witness.* I put the car in reverse, and this time, I slowly pulled out of the driveway and back down Lizardville Road. I was determined to find these boys. I cruised slowly with the same results.

I shook my head and drifted into Tom's General Store. I placed the car in park and opened my door.

"Everything okay, Bob?" Tom said as he approached.

"I need you to see something," I said. Tom looked puzzled. "Can you close the store and come to the house for a few minutes?" I begged.

"I'm running a business here," Tom replied.

"Please, it's important."

"Okay, give me a few minutes." Tom walked back inside the store. I watched as he turned the orange "closed" sign around to face the front of the store. Then he flicked the lights off and locked the door. "I hope this is worth me losing money," Tom added.

"I promise you it is." I started the car and pushed the pedal to the floor.

"Slow down, hot rod, or you will kill us both." Tom quickly frowned. "I'm sorry, I didn't mean that."

"It's okay, I deserve that," I said, slowing the car to an average speed. Tom was right. I was driving like a lunatic. I didn't let that hurt my feelings, even though it felt like a knife piercing my heart when it rolled off Tom's lips.

"So, what happened that I have to see?" Tom begged.

"You'll see," I mumbled as I entered my driveway.

I rolled the car to a stop and quickly popped out the door. Tom followed me to the porch. I whipped the keys from my pocket but remembered I had never locked it when I went after the boys. "See?" My hand trembled as I gave the door a shove. Tom could see for himself what those boys had done to my house. Now, he would understand the urgency and the reason I was so angry and upset.

"What am I looking at?" Tom questioned.

"What? Don't you see? It's right there." I pointed to the coffee table.

"Okay, it's a baseball and baseball glove." Tom looked puzzled.

"You're not getting it, are you?" I pointed again. "That's Bobby's ball and glove!"

"So, you drug me over here to show me Bobby's glove?" Tom was still puzzled.

"Try to follow. I left your store, and while driving home, I spotted two teenage boys walking away from my house with fishing gear. Something wasn't right about it, and I felt it the minute I saw them," I said in desperation. "I parked my car and opened the door to find this." Once again, I pointed to Bobby's glove. "I didn't get this out. Those boys had to have done it. I'm sure of it," I added.

"You made me come here because you think some kids broke into your house, found Bobby's glove, and laid it on the coffee table to mess with you?"

"Yes, now you understand!" I yelled with joy.

"Bob, I think you have officially lost it." Tom shook his head. "You want to blame others when the answer is staring you right in the face." Tom pointed to the glove.

"What are you talking about? I was confused.

"Let me be honest with you. You know my family history with my mother and grandmother. Well, maybe you should consider the unexplained, the supernatural." Tom's beady eyes drilled into me, giving me the creeps.

"Are you talking about ghosts?" I almost choked. *Tom's family was a bit strange, and I never really bought into the whole voodoo thing or the paranormal side of his family. We all have our own beliefs.*

"If you just came over to make fun of me, then I'll take you back to your store." I walked to the front door and out on the porch. Tom followed me to the car. The drive was quick, and neither of us said anything. I dropped him off. I thanked him for taking the time, and I hoped to see him Sunday to watch the baseball game.

I thought about what Tom had said as I returned to the house. *Is it possible that Bobby and April were haunting my house? Was Bobby trying to send me a message? Was this because he loved baseball?* I was not sure I would ever know the answer to that.

Tom showed up Sunday as promised, and the Phillies started the season with a win. Tom never mentioned the paranormal or ghosts to me. I think he knew I was a non-believer.

EIGHT

Monday, October 15, 1962

Most Mondays, I would be at work with the hood up and a wrench in my hand. I loved tinkering with cars, well engines. They fascinated me, even brakes and almost everything on a car or truck. There was something about them. *How did they work?* It was my passion. My dad always said when you find the one thing you love, do it to the best of your ability. When the other mechanics couldn't solve something, they would turn to me. I always loved a good mystery, and after I solved the problem, everyone knew I was the best.

My boss and even the customers loved me. Maybe that was why I got to sleep in today. I wished that were the case. No, today was a special day for me. They didn't want me working. I think I would rather be at work. It would give me something to distract my mind.

Today was Bobby's birthday. He would have been eleven. I should have always taken the day off work for his birthday. We could have spent the day together—Father-and-Son Day, we would have called it. I could have taken him fishing in the morning and bowling in the afternoon. Or tossed the ball around in the yard for a little while. Maybe even taken him to a picture show and stopped for pizza at his favorite place—the Snack Shack.

These are all things I should have done, but I didn't. Because I loved my job. I loved hanging out with the guys. Shop talk, they called it. I think my friends meant more to me than my family. I indeed hung out with them more than with April and Bobby. Maybe I took Bobby and April for granted. I always thought they would be here. April and I would live to be old, happy grandparents. Bobby would grow up and marry the love of his life. *Well, none of that is going to happen. Not now, anyway. I ruined that.*

I lay in bed this morning thinking of everything I should have done, feeling guilty because I didn't. I should have put my family first. The job is a source of money to provide for our family. Yes, do your job well. But always put your family first. That's what I tell the young dads I talk to at the garage.

Today was the first anniversary of "The Crash"— The night that changed my life forever. The night some dumb teenage boy decided to drink and drive. I swear that if I see another underage young man drinking, I might give him a good shove and tell him to smarten up. Alcohol is not the answer to solving any issue and is not the best way to have fun. Heck, chances are you won't remember what you did anyway. I should know. I used to drink when I was young, too. Sometimes, Tom and I would sneak a couple of beers out of his parents' store and drink them in the woods. But I never got behind the wheel of a car and tried to drive when

I was a teenager. *I don't miss beer.* I hadn't had a drink in over a year. I was proud of myself.

"Breakfast is ready!" April shouted. I heard Bobby's footsteps run down the hallway. Laughter echoed from the kitchen. My heart nearly leaped out of my chest. I leaned forward, and a faint slit of light shone through the bottom of the door. I'd always liked sleeping with the door closed. I kicked my legs over the side of the bed and eased my feet into my slippers. I walked to the door. My heart was racing. I turned the knob and wobbled into the hallway when I heard Bobby's voice. I steadied myself against the wall. I glanced back to the bed; April's side was untouched. I could listen to April and Bobby talking. "I hope you're hungry," she said to Bobby.

"I sure am," Bobby answered.

I pinched my arm. Ouch, that hurt. My cheek was wet. This was impossible.

"Dad, are you coming?" Bobby shouted for me to join them. My lip quivered. Tears dripped to the floor. I wiped my face on my pajama sleeve and took a step forward. I don't understand why I was afraid.

"Bo-b-b-y," I stuttered. His bedroom door was open as I passed. *I keep it closed to hide my pain. I need to be brave,* I reminded myself. I closed my eyes, took a deep breath, and walked to the kitchen. Bobby was looking directly at me; I froze at the sight. April was leaning over the counter. I loved seeing them, but I wouldn't say I liked this part because I don't believe in ghosts. *So, how do I explain what I'm seeing?*

April spun around. "There you are. I made you pancakes." She smiled and held the plate outward for me to see.

My eyelids fluttered. Next, I was lying on the kitchen floor. A sharp pain pierced the back of my head. I moved my right hand to my head and rubbed a tender spot. I gazed at the empty kitchen. Bobby and April had vanished. I knew this was impossible. *Had I been sleepwalking?* That's something I have never done before. *Is it possible to start something new as you get older? Did I see Bobby and April? Was that really April? Yes, it was. I would recognize her anywhere.* Maybe I dreamt they were here because I miss them so much, perhaps because it's the first anniversary since they were taken from me.

I placed my hand on the wall and forced myself to stand. My legs grew weak, and my lip twitched again. I pressed my back to the wall to steady myself. *This was impossible.* I cried. *I'd lost my mind.* "Bobby!" I wailed. The floodgates opened. I don't know how long I had been leaning against the wall. All I know is that I had run out of tears. I swallowed hard and took a step toward the table. I stared, not sure if what I was seeing was real. I extended my shaking hand, nerves on end, and I touched the milk in Bobby's Flintstones cereal bowl. I yanked my hand back and watched as the cold milk dripped from my fingers. It was real. I couldn't breathe. The room spun rapidly. It reminded me of those old carnival rides that turned around. I gripped the back of the chair. I didn't want to pass out again. I inched the chair out before I lowered myself. My breathing became erratic. I rested my forehead on the table and closed my eyes.

"It's okay, Dad." Bobby rubbed my back in a circular motion.

I jolted my head back and jumped to my feet. I spun to see an empty room.

"Calm down," April's voice whispered. "You know how you get. Relax and take a deep breath."

My eyes grew wide, and the veins swelled in my neck. I staggered to the couch. *I'm going nuts. I'm seeing and hearing things that are not real.* My body shuddered, and my heart throbbed. I leaned forward as I ran my hands through my hair. *Relax, and take deep breaths.* I inhaled over and over. *That's it, one more time.*

"That's better, dear." I felt her soft touch on my shoulder. I tugged at my hair and let out a scream. I wasn't sure how that was going to help, but for a moment, I did feel better.

I convinced myself this had to be a dream. I knew Tom was coming over after work, but I wasn't sure I could wait that long. Right now, I needed to keep it together. I stared at the table. *The milk and the cereal bowl were both real. But how did the bowl get out of the cupboards, filled with milk, and on the kitchen table? Were April and Bobby living in the house? Were they ghosts? I needed to talk to Tom now!* His family knew about things like this. I'd heard some of his crazy stories. Now, I wasn't sure if they were crazy or not.

I scooched toward the end of the couch and picked up the phone on the end table. I placed my index finger in the five-hole and rotated my hand to the right. Next was the seven, followed by the four. *Just two more sevens and a three and two.* I lifted the handset to my ear and waited.

"Tom's General Store, how can I help you?"

"Tom, Tom, it's Bob. Hurry, I need you," I spat the words out faster than I expected.

"Bob, is that you?"

"Yes, hurry, please."

"Calm down. Tell me, what's going on?"

"Bobby and April are here." I hung up the phone. *Tom must think I'd gone over the edge. Why did I even call him? Oh gosh, what had I done?*

I sat and stared at the ceiling. *I needed to clean the cobwebs in the corner. How come I never noticed them before? How odd to be thinking about that at a time like this.*

The minutes passed, and there came a knock at the door. I glanced in that direction. The knock was louder the second time. "I'm coming in!" Tom shouted, using his key and pushing the door open.

Tom's eyes bore into mine from the doorway. "What's going on that you had to call me on Monday morning?"

I bowed my head. "I don't know."

"You don't know." The tone in his voice was sharp as Tom took a step back and crossed his arms.

"I don't want to sound like a lunatic." I cowered down.

"Bob, I've known you my entire life, the good and the bad. Please tell me what was so urgent that you had to call me this morning?" He stood before me.

I patted the cushion beside me. Tom took his seat next to me. I opened my heart, explaining every detail I could remember about the last hour. Tom nodded and rubbed his chin a few times as he listened intently. I wasn't sure if he believed me, but he remained calm for the entire story.

"I knew today was going to be difficult," Tom said as he patted my shoulder. "But I didn't expect Bobby and April to show up. But it makes sense."

"None of this makes sense. They both died a year ago," I struggled to say.

"But it does. April and Bobby were taken before their time and have unfinished business. That is what holds them here." Tom assured me that this was normal in the spirit world and that he would help me through this tough time.

I had difficulty believing in things I couldn't explain or see. *What did I see? Did I see Bobby and April? Were they still here, living with me?* Tom spent most of the day with me. We chatted about ghosts and the supernatural. I wasn't ready to get on the paranormal bus just yet. I thought most of this was my mind playing tricks on me. I guess time would tell.

NINE

Saturday, November 16, 1962

I woke up and felt pressure next to me. I sat up and swore April was lying beside me for a split second. I rolled out of bed, my alarm clock showing 7:15 a.m. I turned my ear to the kitchen. The house was quiet. *Maybe I should get a dog. No, no pets. I could barely take care of myself. But it would be nice to have some company.*

I had enough time to get cleaned up, so I hopped in and grabbed a quick shower to start my day. The hot water felt nice as it trickled down my body. Sometimes, I wanted to stand here and enjoy the warmth. It's so relaxing. I couldn't stay in the shower for too long. I was expecting Tom and his mother today. I grabbed the faucet handle and turned to the left. I cracked the glass door, grabbed my towel, and dried myself. I wrapped the towel around me and slid the door open.

A chill ran down my spine, and I froze. My mouth hung open, and my eyes welled. My lip quivered, and my body began to shake as I looked at the heart shape drawn on the steamed mirror on the medicine cabinet. Inside the heart was a smiley face—something April would do when she was alive. I never told anyone that, not even Tom. That was one of our little secrets. This told me April was here, still living with me. If April was here, then there was a good chance Bobby was here, too. I'm not crazy, after all.

I stepped forward, placing my hand in the middle of the heart. A wave of energy riveted my body. I backed away, my eyes wide as I leaned against the bathroom wall.

Slowly, I twisted the door handle and opened the bathroom door. I watched as the room temperature cooled to match the rest of the house. The image slowly faded. *April was sending me a message… that she still loved me, even after the accident. I didn't deserve her. I never did, actually. I never knew what she ever saw in me. Maybe it was to get back at her parents for some reason. It didn't matter to me. I loved her, too.*

Some of the things Tom mentioned a month ago were absurd. But then again, how could I explain recent events that I witnessed? How could I explain today? I couldn't explain why Bobby and April were still here. Or were they? Was this real, or was I losing my mind? I needed to stop doubting myself. I wasn't crazy. Maybe I should start drinking beer. No, that wouldn't fix anything.

The thought of believing in ghosts bothered me. I'd never been religious; I went to church to please April. That's what married people do. They compromise. But ghosts… spirits who never crossed over? I guess if one was accurate, the other had to be authentic. I needed proof, yet I had all the evidence I needed. It was staring me right in the face.

That's why Tom was bringing Gladys over to help me understand what was happening and why. I'd known Tom's mom since I was a child. As I got older, I avoided Gladys. She was strange, bizarre, an odd duck. Call her what you want, here she was coming to my house. I couldn't remember the last time I saw her. Tom said Gladys was a medium, a person who could talk to the dead. That sounded like a circus trick to me.

My fingers stopped shaking, and I needed to get some clothes on before they arrived. I returned to my bedroom and slipped on my jeans, a gray t-shirt, and one of my favorite flannel shirts to keep me warm. I made my way toward the kitchen. I stopped in the hallway and took one last look at the mirror. It was clean, with no trace of the heart. *Did I see the heart?* I took a few more steps and paused at the thermostat. I turned the temperature up two degrees. I didn't want Gladys to be cold. She was eccentric, always wearing long black dresses and black work boots with large, thick heels in the back. It didn't stop there. Her gray, frizzy hair was the icing on the cake. Sometimes, she would wear a black hat to match the outfit. Come to think of it, I couldn't recall her wearing any other color. It was always black.

Some local wives, mothers, and ladies in the community went to Gladys for spiritual guidance. She was a fortune-teller. I think she read cards, too. That was how she made her living. What I found bizarre was she could see someone's future, yet she could barely see without her Coke bottle glasses. I guess it's in her mind.

I should feel lucky. Gladys wasn't charging me for the visit. But I was sure of one thing: she would turn my house into a three-ring circus. I had no one to blame but myself because I agreed to allow her to help.

I put two slices of bread in the toaster and a pot of coffee on. The window shade sprang upward in a clatter. I jumped a foot off the ground. I wouldn't say I liked it when that happened. But it happened more than I cared to admit. I needed to replace that one. I left the window shade up. I leaned forward to take in the view. A layer of frost covered the yard, steam rising off the creek as it rippled past the house. It was so peaceful living out here with no neighbors for a mile on either side.

The toast sprang up, and I jumped again. My nerves were on edge this morning. I poured a cup of coffee, buttered my toast, and enjoyed a few moments of silence.

I washed the dishes and tidied up so Gladys would not think I was a slob. I turned on the television and sat on the couch. I crossed my legs, then uncrossed my legs. I fluffed the pillow, then fluffed it again. "Relax," I whispered to myself. *Why was I so nervous?*

It was only Tom and his mom. You would think I never had anyone over before. Okay, a woman hasn't been in the house since April passed. That had to be it.

A knock at the door startled me. I glanced in that direction. It wasn't even ten yet. "Come in," I hollered.

The door inched open, and Tom poked his head inside. "Bob, we're a little early." He eased forward, followed by Gladys, carrying a shoulder bag. She didn't disappoint me. I wanted to tell her Halloween was over. She stopped a few steps in, gazed around, and started to hum.

Tom sat in the recliner and gave me a nod. Gladys's eyes sprang open, and she stepped forward and turned the TV off. "I need silence," she said, her voice raspy.

"I guess we're starting?" I asked.

"Silence," she barked and closed her eyes and began to hum and mumble something.

I looked at Tom, who was staring at me, and he raised a finger to his lips to hush me. I sat and watched the old lady hum and wave her hands in slow, circular motions. First, she faced in the direction of the kitchen, followed by the living room, and then down the hallway. I watched as she went in and out of both bedrooms. "You missed the bathroom and the back porch," I snickered under my breath.

"I feel two lost souls," she announced, stopping in the center of the living room. "The tension is high, and they have something to say." I gazed at Gladys. That was easy for her; she knew April and Bobby were gone. She was at their funeral. I wasn't impressed, not yet anyway. I needed her to make April and Bobby show themselves and talk with them if she wanted me to believe. She paraded to the kitchen counter. She placed both hands on the stove, then the counter and refrigerator. "April spent much time here. She loved cooking for her family." Gladys smiled. She then turned to face me. "Bring me a piece of her clothes and something special to Bobby." I bounced to my feet, darting down the hallway into my bedroom. I flung the closet door open and opened a box with some of her belongings that I didn't donate to charity. I picked up her favorite necklace, wedding ring, and pink sweater. I dashed to Bobby's room and grabbed his baseball glove. These brought back some of my favorite memories.

I laid them on the coffee table. Gladys looked at them from a distance, spending a minute or so on each item before moving closer. She hovered her hands, moving them in a back-and-forth motion, but never touched the objects.

I noticed Gladys's eyes had turned a dark shade of black. "How can she see anything?" I mouthed the words to Tom.

"She just does." He appeared as puzzled as I was. We sat and watched in amazement. The show went on for the next five minutes. Then I finally noticed she was staring directly at me.

"It was you," Gladys blurted out. My lips quivered at her accusation.

"Mom, what are you talking about? We're here to talk to April and Bobby." Tom was at a loss for words.

"I have spoken to them," Gladys whispered.

"How convenient is that?" *I knew this would be a waste of my time.*

Gladys walked over, opened her bag, and pulled out some incense. She then walked in circles around the room, strategically placed a holder, slid in incense, and struck a match to light the end. I watched the smoke rise; the aroma quickly filled the air. The pungent odor irritated my eyes. After the last one was lit, she signaled Tom and me to rise and join her in the middle.

Once the three of us were in the circle, she offered us her hands. I extended my left hand toward her, and I took Tom's in my right. "April and Bobby, please join us," she mumbled repeatedly.

I closed my eyes as Tom had done, but after several minutes, nothing was happening. A sharp chill came over me. My eyes popped open. The temperature dropped, sending shivers down my spine. A few lights twinkled above our heads.

"She's here," Gladys announced as the lights grew brighter.

"Where?" My eyes frantically danced around the room, looking for April and Bobby. Tom nodded upward, and I looked at the twinkling lights. "I see lights," I said, disappointed. I frowned. The lights moved in odd formations, almost hypnotic.

Gladys's chanting grew louder and faster. Her raspy voice was taxing on my ears. "I'm sure the spirits will show up to tell you to be quiet," I snickered under my breath. The light show continued, my eyes burned, and a tear trickled down my cheek. *Would I ever be able to get this stink out of my house*? The lights blinked in and out a few times, then vanished.

Gladys froze, and I felt her eyes burning into my skull. I glanced in her direction, and she looked pissed. Her wide eyes drilled through the back of my head. She unexpectedly released my hand. "Non-believer!" She spun around and capped the first incense, collected them individually, and placed them back into her bag.

"Mom, stop," Tom begged. "Mom, please. We have to help," Tom continued.

"He mocks me, laughs at me, I know. I feel and hear it," she hissed, placing the last container into her bag. She zipped it shut and was out the door before I knew what had happened.

"What did you do?" Tom barked at me.

"Nothing," I exclaimed. I was not too fond of the sound in Tom's voice. *Could she have known what I was thinking? That would be impossible. Did I cause the lights to leave? Was it April or Bobby?* I dismissed them all. "Thanks for trying," I added.

"Let me talk to her," Tom said. "You realize we are your best hope in solving this?"

"Don't waste your time." I shook my head.

The door closed behind Tom. I watched as they pulled away and drove out of sight. *This is just how I envisioned the day would go. She was a fraud. Why the townsfolk believed her, I didn't know. Yet, how do I explain the light show? Why was I seeing April and Bobby?* It had to be my mind playing tricks on me. That was the only logical explanation.

TEN

Friday, April 13, 1963

I t's been almost six months since Gladys tried to summon the spirits in my house. According to Tom, she would never come back. I was baffled and amazed at the same time. Tom repeated word for word what I was thinking that day. Maybe the old coot had a little magic in her after all.

Today is one of those superstitious days. It's Friday the 13th. Instead of being alone, I invited Tom over for lunch. He agreed but mentioned he couldn't be away from the store for too long, especially on a Friday. I understood that running a store by yourself was a significant challenge.

Once in a while, I would work an afternoon at the store so Tom could have some time away. I even suggested he hire someone part-time in the evenings. It would be better than closing altogether. He kept telling me it's something he'd been thinking about.

I perked up when I heard the car door slam. Moments later, the door opened, and Tom strolled in. "Hey, Tom," I said, looking over my shoulder and watching our lunch because I didn't want to burn the hamburgers. "They're almost done. Do you want cheese on yours?"

"That sounds great." Tom placed a bag and an interesting, small wooden box onto the table.

I laid a slice of cheese on top of each hamburger and scooped them up, swiftly tossing them onto the plate. These past two years have taught me a lot. I turned the knob on the stove to make sure the flame went out. I grabbed the plate and moved it to the table. Tom set two bottles of Pepsi onto the table and brought a bag of Middleswarth potato chips to snack on.

I opened the refrigerator and picked up the bowl of Amish potato salad I made last night, as well as my famous purple pickled eggs and beets. I know Tom and I both loved them.

"The burgers are good." Tom smiled as he took a second bite.

"Thanks, they are pretty juicy." I was proud of myself.

"I still prefer them on the grill," Tom said.

"I agree, but I'm not setting the grill up for two hamburgers," I said with a wry smile. There was something about that wooden box that intrigued me. The size of it… the carving on the side… "Whatcha got there?" I pointed to the small chest while stuffing a spoonful of potato salad into my mouth.

"It's something Mom gave me a few weeks ago." Tom smiled.

"Does it open?" I was curious as to what was inside.

"I don't know." Tom looked puzzled.

"What do you mean you don't know?"

"I haven't opened it yet."

"Well, open it!"

"I don't know how." Tom sighed.

"Have you tried?" I was getting anxious.

"Of course, I tried." Tom sounded frustrated.

"Can I see it?" I extended my hand.

"Sure." Tom gently placed the box into my hand.

The hairs stood on the back of my neck. A shiver ran down my spine. I was mesmerized by the touch of the soft wood and the detailed carvings. I rubbed my fingers up and down the top and sides. I pushed with my thumbs along the side walls, hoping to find a way to open the box.

"Did your mom ever open the box?" I gazed at Tom.

"She never said."

"Did you ask her?"

"No, I didn't think to ask," Tom snapped.

"Why not?" I questioned. Tom could tell I was intrigued by this object.

"I don't know. I stopped to say hi and ensure my mom was doing okay. I noticed the box on the table and asked her what it was. She said it was a puzzle box." Tom extended his hands to his sides.

"That's it? It's a puzzle box!" *How could he not ask questions?* That baffled me.

"Yes, that's it." He frowned. "No, wait." He stared at the ceiling. "I did ask her where she got it." Tom smiled, pleased that he did ask a question.

"And?"

"And what?"

"Did she tell you where she got the box?" I couldn't believe I had to drag the information out of Tom. I would have beat the information out of him if I was younger. But

I'm older now and know better. I took another bite of my cheeseburger.

Tom stared at the ceiling a little more. "Mom said the box has been in the family for many years. Dating back to the turn of the century." He nodded. She also mentioned it contained a family secret, a treasure map of sorts."

"Treasure?"

"Yeah." Tom paused. "Not one of riches, but to a family secret."

"What kind of secret?" I needed to know more.

"I don't know. She never told me."

"Call her." I stared at Tom's eyes.

"What? Like now?"

"Yes, now."

"Are you insane?" Tom asked.

"Maybe. I mean, there are days when I feel like I have lost my mind. So maybe I am. After all, I still see April and Bobby in the house, and it's been almost two years." I stopped to wipe a trickle from my eye. *Every time I thought of them, I got choked up. I guess the pain would never go away.*

Tom pushed his chair back, walked to the sofa, sat down, picked up the phone, and began dialing. He placed the phone to his ear. The seconds ticked away, and my heart began to race.

"Hello, Mom." Tom paused to listen. "Hey, I have a few questions about the box you gave me. Okay, okay, I stand corrected. The box I borrowed." Tom gritted his teeth at me.

I chuckled softly.

"Ah-ha, ah-ha." He nodded. "I see. Well, that's interesting." He smiled at me. "I sure will, okay. Thank you, Mom. Love you. Bye." Tom stood, strolled to the table, and glanced at me. He pulled out his chair and took his seat. He gazed at me again, picking up his fork and shoving it into the potato salad.

"Enough, please tell me what she said," I snapped at Tom.

"Really, Bob? I'm trying to help you," Tom said and shot me an evil eye.

"I'm sorry." I wasn't. But I wondered what she had to say. After all, Tom never asked her any questions.

"Well, Bob, she told me," Tom paused and smiled, "to tell you, if you have questions, you need to stop by the house, apologize for what happened last time, and she might consider answering your questions." Tom grinned.

"What the? I didn't mistreat her. Man, that sucks." I pushed back from the table. I grabbed the bottle of Pepsi and guzzled it down. I picked up my plate and set it in the sink. I turned to look at Tom. I gritted my teeth and bit my lip, not wanting to say anything else that would upset him.

"Mom said that would rattle your cage." Tom smiled. "Listen, take my advice. Swing by her house, say sorry, and be genuine. I'm sure she will answer your questions."

"Go with me?" I begged. *I didn't want to be in the house alone with Gladys. The place reeked with the smell of incense. Not to mention, her skull collection creeped me out. I mean, who collects skulls?*

"Maybe tomorrow," Tom agreed. "I'm curious, too!"

ELEVEN

Saturday, April 14, 1963

After a restless night of sleep, I pulled myself out of bed. I tackled my morning chores, showered, and prepared for the day. I glanced at the clock and realized the morning had slipped away. I opened the refrigerator and pulled out the Lebanon bologna and cheese. I grabbed the loaf of bread from the counter, then spread out a napkin and proceeded to make a sandwich. I returned to the fridge for ketchup and milk, sat at the table, and ate lunch.

The puzzle box was eating at my insides. *Who made it? Why was it made? And what secret lay within?* I had to know what it contained. I could not get this out of my head. I knew I needed to speak to Gladys to fill in the blanks. That's if the old bird would talk to me or tell me the truth. The way I treated her, why would she help me with anything?

I needed to be nice to her today. I took a drama class in high school because I thought it would be easy. It turned out to be one of the hardest things I ever did. I have a ton of respect for actors. But, with some luck, that class would help me now. I could put on a performance that would convince Gladys that I was sincere. I only needed to focus.

I put the last piece of the sandwich into my mouth, then guzzled my milk. I rose, placing the glass in the sink. It could wait until later. I glanced at the clock and knew it was time to head over and see Tom.

Early to midafternoon was always a slow time at the General Store. I needed Tom to go with me. I felt it would help ease the tension. I grabbed my wallet and car keys off the nightstand and headed outside. I paused in the living room. There was Bobby's baseball glove and ball on the coffee table. I was getting used to seeing weird and unusual happenings around the house. Sometimes, it was a strong smell, and other times, it was objects being moved. Today, I didn't have time. I smiled and closed the door behind me. I knew Bobby was sending me a message, and I was all right with that.

Spring had arrived, and everything was in full bloom. I drove slowly to the store, enjoying the sights on my Saturday drive. I noticed a man fly fishing in the creek. I flashed back to my younger years. I had always meant to take Bobby fishing. Heck, we could have even done that in the backyard—had a little campfire burning in the evening hours. We had the perfect spot. I guess there were a lot of things I meant to do. It's funny how quickly time flies. Now, I regret the missed opportunities. I crossed the bridge and pulled into the side parking lot. Walking to the front, I stopped to listen to the birds chirping in the trees. What a peaceful day; if I could only get Gladys to tell me everything I needed to know, this would have been perfect.

I turned the corner, and Tom sat on the bench in front of the store. Funny, because he wasn't sitting there a minute ago when I pulled up. I didn't need any more mysterious things happening today. Of course, Tom held a bottle of Pepsi in each hand. I smiled and took the bottle from him as he extended his hand.

"Thanks, Tom." I chuckled. *He loved his soda, and I was just as guilty.* "How are you today?" I asked.

"It's a perfect day. Spring is one of my favorite times." Tom grinned. "Hey, did you hear? William Parker bought the house across the street from the Axe Factory."

"No, I hadn't heard that. In fact, I didn't know it was up for sale." I guess I was no longer in the town gossip circle. That was more of April's thing than mine.

"Gosh, do you remember the time we went up the Basket Maker Hallows and hiked to the top of the mountain?" Tom said.

"Of course, I could never forget that. We spent the entire day hiking, and oh, do you remember the pond and little waterfall we found?" My excitement level grew.

"Oh, gosh, yes. That was a neat little place." Tom's eyes grew wide. "How about the cave we found?" Tom's eyes locked with mine as we nodded together.

"Oh my, I had forgotten all about the cave. That place gave me the willies," I said.

"You felt it, too?" Tom asked.

"Of course," I said.

"You never said anything. Why not?"

"We were kids. We all acted like we were tough guys," I snickered. "Honestly, we were just a couple of scared kids exploring a cave."

Tom looked at me, then over to the creek. "I suppose you're right." He tapped his finger on the side of the bottle.

"I know I'm right." I gave Tom a sidelong glare. "So, do you want to hike to the top of the mountain and explore the cave today?"

"Are you crazy?" Tom chuckled. "I can't hike up there without losing my breath. I'm not a kid anymore. Besides, we should go to my mother's so you can get the apology over with," Tom said.

"Nothing like getting straight to the point." I furrowed my brow.

"I didn't mean to rain on your parade, but I think you're stalling," Tom said.

"Hey," I threw my hands up. "You're the one who brought up the past." I rose to my feet.

"So, I take it you're ready?" Tom added.

"Sure, let's get this over with."

"That's the spirit, Bob. I'm sure Mom would love to help you with that attitude," Tom smirked.

I kept my mouth shut most of the way to Gladys's. I enjoyed the cool spring air hitting my face and ruffling what hair I had left. Tom signaled and turned down Water Street. Gladys's home came into view. A chill ran up my spine. I was feeling anxious. I'd known this woman my entire life, but I felt on edge about this meeting. I took a deep breath and exhaled.

"Are you alright?" Tom snickered.

"I'm fine," I snapped back.

Tom just smiled as we pulled into the driveway. The car slowed and jerked to a halt. I inhaled again and pulled on the door handle. My hand twitched. *Dang, why was I so nervous?* I shook my head, walked behind Tom to the door, and followed him inside. Gladys appeared from the kitchen and gave Tom a friendly hug. She glanced at me and smiled.

"Do you boys want something to drink?"

"I'm good," Tom replied.

Gladys looked at me. "Ah, no, thank you, ma'am." *Why did I say ma'am*? I blushed.

"I've known you since you were that size of a crayfish, and you pick today to start calling me ma'am? Relax, dear. Sit down and let me get you two something to drink." Gladys spun and disappeared into the kitchen. I heard the refrigerator open and close, followed by a hissing sound, then another. She entered, carrying a Pepsi in each hand. She hovered over the two of us with a Pepsi in each hand. "Coasters, please," she barked. *Now I know where Tom got his Pepsi addiction.*

Tom and I quickly grabbed a coaster and slid them onto the coffee table. At the same time, Gladys placed the bottle on each of them. She smiled and eased into the recliner and gazed directly at me. "What would you like to say to me, Bob?"

"Oh, ah. Thank you for the soda." Her sudden question caught me off guard. She must be reading my mind again; I wouldn't say I like it when she does that.

"Anything else?" She gritted her teeth as Tom quickly nudged me.

"Oh, yes." I inhaled. "I'm sorry for doubting you and your abilities." I wiped the sweat from my palms to my jeans.

"Now, ya see. That wasn't so hard, was it?" Gladys said.

"No, ma'am…" I stopped. "No, Gladys." I smiled.

"Now, how can I help you today?" She smiled.

I forgot I had questions for her. Now, if I could only remember them. Why was this so hard? "Um, the puzzle box," I choked out. "Where did the box come from?"

"Well, that's a complicated question, dear," Gladys rubbed her chin, giving the question some thought. "It goes back to the turn of the century, almost sixty years ago. My great-grandmother hid something in the box and placed a spell on the contents to keep it safe. My mother told me the box contained a family secret when she left it to me. Now, I passed the box to Tom for safe keeping." She gazed at the two of us. "But remember, the box contains a family secret; you must not tell a soul about the box. Bob, you are part of this family and must guard the box with your life. Do you understand?" Gladys's eyes darted back and forth.

"But..." I sputtered. "What's the secret?"

"Well, if I knew, that would mean I could open the box, and I haven't." Gladys loved this game she was playing.

"Are you saying you never opened the box?" I had to watch my thoughts; I couldn't take the chance of upsetting Gladys again.

"You are correct, Bob." Gladys sighed. "I'm not sure what you boys are up to, but you don't want to mess with this box. I don't know what lies inside, but I can feel something. It's a strong force. It's not good. My best guess is the secret could lead to a great discovery or open a window to the past. You don't want to open any windows." Gladys frowned.

I watched as Gladys sank into her chair. "So why did you give the box to Tom?"

Gladys rolled her eyes at me. "Have you not paid attention?" Her eyes drilled through me. "The box belongs to the Evans family. Our family! Tom is next in line; one never knows how long one will live, and I can't risk having the box fall into the wrong hands."

"Mom, are you dying?" Tom interrupted, stunned.

"We're all dying, son." Gladys shook her head. "From the day we are born, Death will follow." She gave us each a sidelong stare. "Now, if you don't have any more questions, I would like to turn on the telly and watch my new game show, *Let's Make a Deal* with Monty Hall. He's a handsome fellow." She smiled and blinked a few times.

"Really, Mom." Tom shook his head.

"Thank you for the soda pop and for answering my questions," I said and stood.

"Shhh." Gladys shooed me and Tom away, her eyes fixed on the TV.

TWELVE

Saturday, July 20, 1963

The sun pierced the curtains. I should have never built a home where the bedroom was on the east side of the house. *What was I thinking*? I placed a pillow over my head, but I had to face that, once I was awake, there was no going back to sleep. It was something I was never good at. Now, I had to get out of bed and face the day. *April could roll over and fall asleep for another hour or two*. I was not so lucky.

I cleaned up, ate breakfast, and headed to town for a few things. My first stop was to fill up the gas tank. Tom was pretty busy, so we kept our chit-chat to a minimum. I drove down the main street in Mill Hall. Nothing was happening here. I'm not sure what I expected. It was a Saturday morning. When I was a kid, Mom and Dad would bring me here, and we walked around the farmer's market. They had some of the best homegrown veggies.

I slowed and pulled into the A&P grocery store. I parked the car, grabbed a shopping cart, and proceeded inside. I was not too fond of shopping. I mean, I needed food and supplies. But that was something April did. *Maybe I should have gone with her and helped a little more.* There were things you couldn't get back when the one you loved was gone. Time was one of those things.

I turned the corner and started down the next aisle. I paused for a moment. An attractive woman with curly blonde hair pushed a cart toward me. She smiled and pressed her lips together. "Hi Bob, how are you today?" Her voice was cheerful.

She looked so different from the last time I had seen her. She wasn't wearing baggy clothes today. Her blue dress went down to her knees. She looked stunning. She was older than I remember. I caught a glimpse of her brown eyes behind her glasses. *I wished I had put on a better shirt now.* "Hi, Nurse Betty."

"Oh please, call me Betty." Her fingers were soft as she laid her hand on my arm.

"Okay, hi, Betty." I smiled. I felt queasy and weak in the knees. *Maybe Tom was right. I needed to date again. After all, it's been almost two years.* "So, how have you been?

"Oh, you know, working long shifts at the hospital. But I love helping and meeting people." Her smile was mesmerizing. I couldn't help looking at her left hand—no ring on her finger. "How have you been?" She removed her hand from my arm and leaned on her cart.

"Same as you… Working, I mean. At the garage, of course. I'm a mechanic." Why was I nervous? It's not like I haven't talked to a woman before.

"I didn't know you were a mechanic. Well, if I ever have car trouble, I know who to call." She laughed, and our eyes met.

"Of course, you can call me anytime. After all, I owe you my life. Without you, I don't know what I would have done in the hospital. Thank you for everything." My voice was sincere.

"Aw, aren't you the sweetheart? You're welcome. It was a pleasure taking care of you." Betty batted her eyes at me. *It was apparent she liked me. I had to seize the moment.*

"I would love to buy you dinner sometime," I said. She looked surprised. "As my way of saying thank you." I quickly added.

"Did someone say dinner? Lunch would be more like it," Doctor Michael said as he placed two bottles of wine in Betty's cart. "Hey Bob, you are looking pretty good, and I see you are getting around quite well without the cane," Michael said as he extended his hand to mine.

I took his hand firmly in mine. "Good to see you, Doc," I lied. The sting of seeing the two of them together hurt. *Betty had to be in her early to mid-thirties. I was in my early forties, but the doctor had to be in his fifties. She would be better off with me.* I concealed my pain as the doctor wrapped his arm around Betty's back.

"Well, it was great seeing you two. I don't want to take up much of your time. Thank you for everything you both did for me." I waved and pushed my cart forward. I paused halfway down the aisle. I glanced over my shoulder. Betty turned to meet my eyes, giving me a little wave and a sad look. *She must have sensed that I liked her, and dinner was more like a date.* I frowned and went up and down the aisles so I could get everything on my list. I had this down to a science. I passed Betty and Michael a time or two in the store, and then they vanished. I picked up the last few things on my list. I checked out and loaded the car.

"I think she liked you," April whispered.

Frightened, I jumped and looked around to make sure I was alone. I was. *Did I want to hear April's voice? Or was my mind playing tricks on me?*

I drove home, thinking about what could have been between Betty and me, but it wasn't good to dream about things that would never happen. I think April would have approved. I turned my blinker on and rolled down the gravel driveway. *What in the world?*

I spotted a few guys sitting on the bank of the river. They looked at me when I got out of the car. I walked toward them and noticed they were teenage boys. "Hey, what are you doing on my property?" I hollered.

"Relax, daddy-o." The older boy stood and waved. "We're swimming."

"This is my property, and you need to leave now." My blood pressure was rising. *Who did these kids think they were messing with?* I started walking toward them. Three of the boys were clever and grabbed the innertubes and makeshift rafts and pushed off to the center of the creek. "Come on, man, let's get out of here," one of them yelled at the older boy.

"Man, I have every right to be on the water." The older boy stood his ground.

"Maybe, but your feet are on my property, and I don't want to hurt you in front of your friends. So, take a hike, like your buddies." I stepped forward, stopping a few feet from him. He was a tall, skinny kid… sixteen, if I had to guess. He was no match for me. Just cocky, that's all. He was probably trying to show off for his friends. *I didn't need any trouble. But if this kid didn't leave, I would throw him into the water headfirst.*

"Well, old man, whatcha gonna do?" he said in a smart-ass tone as he raised his hands and balled them into fists.

"Son, don't make me throw you off my land." Our eyes locked. "Last chance to leave." I balled my right hand up and pounded it into my left hand a few times. The last thing I wanted to do was hurt this young man. He didn't realize I took boxing at the YMCA when I was young. I had won a lot of fights, too. Once a boxer, always a boxer.

"You don't scare me." He smirked.

"Come on, James!" his friends hollered from the water.

"Listen to your friends, James." My blood boiled, and I flashed back to the night of the car accident. The boy's name was James. I huffed, stepped forward, and watched as he stepped back. I took another step forward, and James did the stupidest thing anyone could do. He lunged at me. I blocked him with my left arm, twisted behind him, pinned his arm behind his back, and walked him to the water's edge. He whimpered the entire way.

With every ounce of strength, I pushed him forward and watched him splash face-first a few yards away. A sharp pain landed on my side. The boys were throwing rocks at me. I stood fast and looked each one of them in the eye. "I know your moms and dads. I went to school with them!" I yelled. Just like that, the rocks stopped. I crossed my arms and stood victorious. These kids didn't know who they were messing with. "I better not see any of you again," I growled, gritting my teeth.

His buddies scrambled to his side, scooping him up and helping him back to one of the innertubes. I picked up the extra innertube and tossed it out into the water. "Get off my land and water and never return," I warned. I grabbed a handful of the stones that lined the bank. I could tell the kids were petrified, and I didn't care. They had no right to be on my property. I thought about throwing the first rock, but something tugged at my arm. I turned, and for a split second, April appeared, giving me a stern look. I could tell she was not happy.

"What are you doing, Bob?" April whispered. The rocks toppled from my hand as my eyes welled up.

I snapped out of my daze when I heard a horn blowing. I gazed back and forth over the creek. The boys were long gone. *How long had I been standing here?* I turned to see Tom parking his car next to mine.

"What were you thinking?" Tom yelled at me.

"What are you talking about?" I was surprised by his accusations.

"You know dang well what I'm talking about. Four boys stopped at my store screaming and yelling about crazy Old Man Smithers. Something about how you started fighting with them, and you even picked one up and threw him into the creek? What is wrong with you? For God's sake, man, they are only kids!"

"They had no business being on my land and snooping around my property." I hung my head. "I warned them, but they wouldn't leave," I whispered. I looked up to see Tom was pretty upset with me. "April wasn't happy with me, either." I shrugged.

"April? What does she have to do with this?"

"They called the older boy James. I guess it triggered something." *I covered well, if I may say so.* I looked up again, and Tom softened.

"Bob," he started to say, shaking his head. He extended his left hand and scratched the back of his head. "Bob," he huffed. "You need to think before you act. Everybody knows you have been through a lot in the past two years. But it's time to put that behind you. Date someone, get a dog. Do something other than work and hide out here in your house. Please, I beg you. Let me know, we can go out one night if you like… maybe catch a movie." He put his hands on his hips and gazed at me.

I nodded; I wasn't sure how to respond. *Tom was the only friend I had. Yes, I knew a group of guys and gals from the car dealership where I worked, but I didn't hang out with them. Maybe Tom was right. I needed a cat or dog, okay, perhaps even a lady in my life.*

"Well, are you going to say something?" Tom asked.

"I'm sorry I lost my cool when I heard his name was James!" I stuttered.

"I think you need to apologize to the boy and his family," Tom suggested.

"Not a chance," I said firmly. "Not a chance." I shook my head.

THIRTEEN

Sunday, July 21, 1963

Startled, I sat up and leaned forward. My room was freezing. I looked at the window; it was closed. The weatherman on TV had called for a lovely day outside in the mid to upper seventies. So why was my room so cold? I rubbed my eyes, pulled the blanket to my chin, and lay back on my pillow.

"Bob." My eyes popped open. The voice was natural. Not something I had dreamt. "Bob," April whispered. I recognized her voice.

I pushed back into the bed. A white cloud-shaped object was sitting on the edge of my bed. My eyes fluttered. It wasn't cloudy anymore. It was April. Time froze and stood still. The seconds ticked away as if everything was happening in slow motion. I gazed at her, mortified by what I was seeing. *What did she want? Why was she here?* "Bob." I watched her lips move as she said my name.

"What," I stuttered. Yes, I would be lying if I said I wasn't frightened. *Could April hurt me? Or better yet, would she?* My stomach felt twisted. I hated feeling nauseated. The fact that I had a spirit sitting next to me on the bed was unbelievable. It's not the first time I had seen her or Bobby. But this time, she was here to talk to me. I suppressed a shiver. "Hi, April."

"Hello, Bob." She glanced sidelong at me.

"Am I dreaming?" I inhaled, then exhaled. "Are you really here?"

"Yes, Bob, but only for a few moments." She frowned.

"I'm sorry for everything, April. I never meant…" April placed a finger to her mouth to silence me.

"What you did yesterday was wrong. I can't believe what I witnessed. You could have hurt that boy. He's only a child." She shook her head. "You need to apologize to him and his family." Her voice was stern.

I cocked an eyebrow. "But April,"

"No," she huffed as she touched my forearm. My skin began to crawl. She was cold. Her touch seared my left arm. I pulled back and startled April.

"What's wrong, Bob?" she hissed.

"I'm sorry, it was too cold to handle." I told the truth. April needed to know that her touch was painful. Her expression changed; her eyes saddened, and she looked away.

"I didn't mean to upset you or hurt your feelings." I glanced upward. She raised her head slightly. She was real, or as real as a ghost could be. She blinked in and out for a second. "What's wrong?" I didn't want her to leave.

"This drains me." She frowned. "I grow weak, and I need to rest. Please, Bob, do the right thing. Please apologize for yesterday." April looked exhausted. "Please, Bob… for me."

She faded. "Please don't go. Don't leave me again. I need you. I started to cry as I watched her evaporate into thin air.

How could she expect me to apologize to that boy for trespassing on my property? And he attacked me first. Why do I have to do it? I ran my fingers over the blanket where April had been sitting. It was still cold to the touch. *This wasn't a dream. It was real. I needed to stay strong. This meant that April and Bobby were still with me.* I smiled briefly. *But were they here? It's not like I could hold her or Bobby in my arms. No, they were gone, and I needed to start by moving on. This couldn't be good for my mental state. I needed to tell April and Bobby it was time for them to move on…cross over…or whatever they did. It was time for them to leave the house and leave me alone…No, I couldn't tell April that. It would hurt her feelings. Besides, Bobby was only a child; he wouldn't understand. I just needed to leave things alone, at least for now.*

"April, I hope you can still hear me. You and Bobby were the best thing that ever happened to me. I love you both, and I always will." I was selfish; I liked having them around, and it was time to protect my secret.

I tossed the blanket to the side. The room had warmed since April left. I guess that was one way to know she or Bobby was present. I slipped my feet into my slippers and moseyed down the hallway to put on a pot of coffee. I slid the kitchen window open, gazed over the river, and watched the water drift past.

I washed up and put my clothes on while the coffee brewed. I returned to the kitchen and noticed one of Bobby's *Dracula* books on the coffee table. *I guess he wanted me to read to him.* I smiled. That would have to wait; first, I needed to guzzle some coffee.

I took a big gulp and almost burnt my tongue. Enjoying the warmth, I wrapped my fingers around the cup. I gazed at the window and listened. The birds chirped in the distance. I could visualize the ripples in the water by the sound. It was so peaceful. This was why I moved out here. I loved the quiet.

My morning was soon interrupted by the crunching of gravel under tires. It was awfully early for Tom to be stopping by. I perked up when I heard a second car door close. There were more than one set of footsteps on the porch—two, possibly three, if my hearing was correct.

I gazed at the clock. It was a little after ten on a Sunday morning. Who would have the nerve to stop by this early and uninvited? The knock at the door came as no surprise. *If I didn't move, they might think I was not home. But my car was out front, so I was sure they would figure it out.* I pushed my chair back and rose to my feet. The tension was high as I moved slowly to the door. *Could it be the local sheriff coming to talk to me about the events of yesterday?* I was getting that funny feeling in my stomach again. *Or was it the boy's father stopping to speak to me or even fight with me for roughing up his son?* I guess there was only one way to find out.

I turned the knob and opened the door. It was James, the boy from yesterday, and I assumed the man and woman standing behind him were his mother and father.

"Can I help you?" I stood tall and tried to steady my voice.

"Hi, mister, I'm not sure you remember me." The poor kid was shaking in his boots.

"Hi," his father mouthed, arms crossed, while standing behind his son. I recognized him from the garage. *Oh, great, one of our customers. The last thing I needed was to get in trouble at work. Please don't panic,* I tried to reassure myself.

"Yes, you're James. We met yesterday over there." I pointed to the side yard next to the water.

"Ah, yes sir, right over there." James pointed in the same direction. "Ah, I'm sorry for trespassing on your land, sir." He swallowed. "I didn't mean you no harm. I swear." Nervous, he swayed from side to side as his eyes welled up.

"It's alright, James. I didn't mean to yell at you boys, either. I could have handled things better." I made eye contact with his mother and father, then returned my focus back to James. "It's just I was startled by you all, and I wasn't sure what you would be doing here except being up to no good." I nodded.

"Mr. and Mrs. Goodson. I'm sorry if I startled your boy yesterday. There were a lot of them and only one of me. I felt threatened. I wanted you to know that."

"Thank you, Mr. Smithers. When our boy told us what happened, I was agitated. Not so much with you, but with James for disrespecting your place and talking back to an adult. We raised him better than that. I also know what happened to your family. I understand his name must not sit well with you."

I could tell Mrs. Goodson wanted to say something but didn't. I was relieved she didn't say anything. "Thank you all for being so understanding, and thank you, James, for apologizing. That's the sign of a good man," I said. This prompted a little smile out of Mrs. Goodson.

"I'm hoping we can put this behind us and move on?" Mr. Goodson said as he stepped forward to shake my hand.

I extended my hand to meet his and gave a nod. "Thank you."

"Thank you. And thank you for your time. We should be getting over to the church. James here needs to do a little extra praying." He freed my hand and gathered his family to the car. I gave a slight wave as he turned around and drove out of sight.

I closed the door behind me, pushed the lock over, and leaned on the door to steady myself. I took a few deep breaths. The temperature plunged, and my eyes popped open. A cloudy mist filled my kitchen. I smiled, waiting for April to appear. *I'm sure she would be happy with how I handled this situation. I even said I was sorry.*

"You look disappointed. That hurts my feelings," a nasty-looking old man said as he manifested before my eyes.

I was confused. The man was dressed from the early nineteen hundreds. I remembered seeing pictures of similar clothes in books. "Who are you?" I managed to say, still shocked that another ghost was in my house. I had no clue who he was. I shivered.

"Just a friendly warning to let you know that boy is up to no good, and he will be back."

"What?" He still hadn't answered my question. "Who are you?"

"You can call me Donald. I'm here to protect you and your family." He had an unsettling, evil laugh. *My world was unraveling, and I had no idea how to prevent it.*

"Why are you here, Donald?" I spoke. "What do you mean, *my family?* I live alone."

"Don't play me for a fool, Bob. I know April and Bobby live here, too. I know everything that happens in my valley. Just know Donald is on your side." He faded as quickly as he appeared, and the heat returned to the room.

Did he refer to himself in the third person? I needed to figure out who Donald was. Did he have a last name? Why did he say his *valley? I think it's time to talk to Tom and Gladys again.*

FOURTEEN

Monday, July 22, 1963

I called Tom and Gladys, who were unavailable yesterday, so I had to wait for them to arrive this evening. I came home from work and entered the door when I heard noises from my bedroom. I hurried down the hall to find an empty room. Then I noticed the hole in the screen and watched as a squirrel scurried away. I hated being on edge every day. I slipped out of my work clothes, quickly showered, and changed into something more comfortable.

Just in the nick of time. I heard car doors slam outside and noticed Tom and Gladys heading to the door. I stepped over and opened it for them.

"Thank you both for coming over," I said humbly. *The last time Gladys was here, things didn't go so well, and I didn't want to have a repeat of that day.*

"I see you have learned from the last time," Gladys snickered. Tom looked puzzled but knew his mom must have seen or felt something.

"So why the urgent call yesterday?" Tom sat on the couch. Gladys walked about with her hands stretched at her sides, and she hummed softly.

"It was a weird day," I started.

"When aren't your days weird?" Tom cut me off and shot me an odd look.

"Nice, really nice." I shrugged my shoulders. "I had two sets of visitors yesterday. First, the Goodsons stopped by. James and his parents." I nodded and explained that visit. Tom approved. I didn't need his approval, but it was nice to have it. "After they left, my day turned in a different direction."

"April, in the morning, then the Goodson family," Gladys interrupted.

"I just said that, Gladys."

"Yes, you did, but I need to know what kind of warning Donald gave you?"

I sank into the recliner. "Um, yeah, how do you do that?"

"Okay, who's Donald?" Tom asked. "Have I met him?" He had no clue.

"That is the million-dollar question on the table. Because I don't know," I added. We both turned our attention to Gladys.

"Donald Thornhill was the original Ax Factory owner in 1904 or 1905, if my memory serves me correctly. No, boys, I was not alive back then. Several years later, I was born." We both giggled like a couple of ten-year-olds. *I wouldn't say I liked that she could read our minds.* "He and his wife, Annabelle, lived across the street. The same house the Parker family recently purchased," Gladys added.

"Are they safe living in that house?" Tom said with concern.

"Only time will tell, so where was I? Yes, Donald had another child with another woman named Samantha Smithers," she whispered.

My mouth dropped. "So, he's my great-great-grandpa?" I said excitedly.

"Something like that," Gladys said, her tone flat. "Donald has an agenda, but I'm not sure it favors you," she said. "He hides many secrets. One must be careful around Donald Thornhill."

"Can you call him?" I begged.

"Were you not listening? I'm not sure we want to do that. Not yet, anyway. Let me do some research, and I will get back to you. If he shows himself again, ask him what he wants with you. Why is he here? How can you help him? Spirits don't show up for fun. They have meaning and a purpose. Tread lightly with this one. He is old and wise," Gladys warned me. I valued her opinion; she always sought my best interest.

"Can I do anything to protect myself if he shows up?" I was a little nervous and didn't want this person, spirit, to try and hurt me. I stared at Gladys.

"Always carry a lot of salt in your pocket. Grab a handful and sprinkle salt around you in a circle if he shows up," Gladys said, giving me a quirky little grin.

"Will that protect me?" I said anxiously. Tom leaned forward to make sure he didn't miss anything.

"I don't know. I read it in a spells book, but I have never had a reason to need salt." She gave me a wry smile. "Let me know if it works, and good luck." Gladys nodded, giving me the wry smile again.

Now she was playing with me. But I would take her advice to heart and carry salt with me. At least it could offer me some sort of protection, I hoped.

"This is all crazy stuff. Who knew ghosts were real?" Tom said.

"I've known ghosts exist since I was a little girl. From the time I was eight years old, my grandma and I would talk about these types of things."

"Do you miss her?" Tom asked.

"Not at all," Gladys added.

"Why not? I miss my grandma." Tom sat up straight, offended by the fact that his mother didn't miss her mother.

"My dear boy, I talk to her once, if not twice, a week. She lives here." She pointed to her heart. "But she also appears to me when I need her. I'm sure she will have much to say about Donald Thornhill." She gazed at Tom, then at me. "Promise me, you will be careful, should he return."

"I promise," Tom and I said in unison. I was fascinated and scared at the same time. I also wondered if April and Bobby were safe. I guess, for now, there was nothing I could do to protect them. Heck, I'm not sure there was anything that anyone could do. They were spirits, and I was only human. Shortly after Tom and Gladys left, I grabbed a small plastic bag from the drawer and filled it halfway with salt. I tied the top and stuffed it in my pocket. *You could never be too safe!*

FIFTEEN

Tuesday, October 15, 1963

I took a week of vacation. Everyone at work understood. This was sure to be a difficult time for me—the second anniversary of the loss of April and Bobby. The day started like any other. I woke, got dressed, had breakfast, and now was sitting in front of the TV.

Startled, I jumped when I heard gunfire in the distance. It was a little early for hunting season. Maybe someone was getting a little practice before deer season began. I was never big on hunting. My father didn't hunt, so I never had a lot of practice shooting a gun. But I could shoot if I needed to! I would sit and watch the deer graze in the yard in the evenings. Soon, one or two of them wouldn't be here. Poor defenseless animals up against a gun or a bow and arrow. It didn't seem fair to me, but I also understood the other side. It provided food for many families in the valley.

My head snapped to Bobby's room. I listened, and I heard the closet door close. My first thought was that it was just some neighbor kid or kids playing a prank on me. *If I ever caught anyone in my house, they would pay the price. I know they didn't like me, and the feeling was mutual.* I dismissed the thought. I stood and walked back to ensure an animal hadn't figured out how to get in the house on such a cold day. The weather was always funny and hard to predict. It was sixty degrees during the day two days ago, and today, the high would only be thirty.

I wrapped my hand around the doorknob. I pulled back to shake the chill from my hand. My anxiety spiked. Bobby must be here. It had been too long since I'd seen him. I gathered my courage, quickly turned the knob, and gently eased the door open a few inches. The room was cold and bleak; a light mist hung in the air. *Had I stepped outside?* Then, I noticed a couple of coloring books and a box of crayons on the floor. I watched in amazement as the lid on the box opened, and a blue crayon slid out, landing on the open page. It moved, standing upright, and began to draw on the spaceship. My eyes welled up, and a tear traced down my cheek. Bobby loved outer space and talked about being an astronaut. It was my fault he would never achieve his dreams.

The blue crayon stopped and fell on the carpet. I heard a bit of a giggle. The red crayon slid out of the box and started to draw on the page. I was puzzled. He was not staying in the lines at all. I looked twice. He was spelling something in the middle of the page — first, a B, followed by the O and two more Bs, and then a Y. The crayon moved a little lower on the page and started moving again. This time, the crayon drew an I and then an S. Bobby is? Bobby is what? I felt off-kilter; I clung to every word. The crayon moved again to the bottom of the page and started a new word, beginning with a capital D. The crayon floated upward about a foot. Bobby is D? "Bobby, what are you trying to say?" I stared at the floor, my breathing shallow and quick.

The crayon didn't move. It hovered in midair about a foot over the open page. "Help me," I heard a young boy's voice whisper.

"Bobby…" My voice quivered. My anxiety rose, and I looked back and forth in the room at a frantic pace. "Bobby, are you alright? Can you hear me? Speak to me." I pushed the door open a little more and poked my head out to make sure he was not hiding behind it. I froze when the crayon started to move again. This time, it etched out a capital E, followed by a red A and then a D. My breathing increased, and I wobbled and steadied myself on the wall. Bobby is DEAD? What? Why? "Bobby, why would you write that?" I questioned, my voice raspy.

Laughter erupted—not a child's voice. No, this was the voice of an older man. Much older. "Bobby's dead." He continued laughing. I shoved the door wide open. I wasn't sure what to do. *The salt*. I untied the bag of salt from my pocket and panicked when the bag slipped from my fingers and spilled onto the floor. How quickly things change when you live in a haunted house. "You killed your son," the voice whispered. "Everyone knows what you did." His laughter continued.

"Who are you?" I asked, even though I thought I had a pretty good idea who this might be. I didn't expect him to respond. I knelt over, grabbed as much salt as possible, and scattered it around me in a circular pattern.

"You know what you have to do?" the voice announced.

"What?" *What do I have to do?*

"You took your son's life. Now, it's time to do the right thing. A life for a life!"

I softened. "Are you asking me to take my own life? Are you telling me Bobby will return if I take my own life?" That was something that never crossed my mind. *Could it be true? Could a powerful spirit send someone back to the living side? That would be impossible.* I'd never heard of anything like that before, except in the tabloid headlines that lined the checkout lanes in the local supermarkets. *"A woman has a two-headed baby." "Husband abducted by aliens." "Man comes back to life." No one believed those newspapers, did they? Were they real or fake?*

"Show yourself, Great-Grandpa." I snapped out of my daze and glanced around the room, waiting to see if Donald Thornhill would show himself. "Show yourself!" I hollered. It's times like this I was thankful I lived out in the country. I was sure my neighbors would have called the local sheriff if I lived in town.

"Show yourself!" I screamed, then exhaled to calm my nerves. "I guess you are scared," I said.

Inside, I shivered with fear, unsure what to do if he showed up. I was counting on the fact that I was his distant relative. Maybe that would keep me alive. Or perhaps the salt had repelled him. "Um…" I rubbed my chin. Part of me wished Tom or Gladys were at my side. It would make me feel safer. But I had an unsettling realization that I needed to do this alone. I raised my eyebrow when a small light appeared over the coloring books. "Oh my gosh," I muttered to myself.

The light grew; my mouth hung open, panic rising within. My breath was heavy in the air. I didn't care how often I saw this or something unexplained; I was still scared.

Maybe because anything could go wrong when dealing with the unexplained. Donald appeared and stood before me. He furrowed his brow and stilled me with a smile. "I had forgotten we were related."

I pursed my lips to suppress my smile. He remembered we were related. That helped me relax a little. "Why are you here?" I choked out. *I needed to pull it together.*

I blinked, and he was standing before me. I could almost smell his breath. *I didn't know spirits could put off an odor. I'll have to remember that for the future.* I scuttled back, and the door slammed behind me. I was trapped like a mouse in a cage. My innards twisted and squirmed. "What do you want?" I managed to spit out. Once again, he closed the gap between us.

"I should have left Annabelle and married Samantha," he declared. He seemed bitter about the choices he had made in his life. *I guess power and money could make you do things you'd regret.* "Don't you have something you wish you could change?" he questioned me. I frowned, knowing exactly what he meant.

"Yes, two years ago today." My voice softened, and I gazed at the floor. A tear rolled down my cheek. "Yes, the pain of losing April and Bobby haunts me daily. Could I have done more? Should I have turned left, not right? I've beat myself up day in and day out for the past two years," I confessed as the pain boiled inside.

"Yes, you have made bad decisions. You ignored your wife and child when they were alive. You can't change that, but I can help." He wagged his finger at me. "See, I ruined my life by making the wrong choice, and I can't change that. Now, you have ruined your life, but I can help you if you desire my help," he said, his voice husky and calm. "All you have to do is ask, and I can take all your pain away."

"Don't listen to him," a female voice whispered. *Or was that me wanting to hear April's voice?*

"I'm listening," I stood up straight.

"Good," he said, smiling.

"Bob, don't listen to him." April's voice filled my head. The room spun. I steadied myself. April's voice grew louder. "Bob, listen to me." I slowly turned to face April, but she was not there.

"It's time for you to go!" April's voice screamed like a massive explosion filled the room. I dropped to my knees and covered my ears as the pain seared.

"I'm not going anywhere without my prize," Donald replied. His voice was tight.

A bright light appeared behind him and shot through Donald like a bullet fired from a gun. He stumbled backward, blinked in and out, and vanished before my eyes. Silence filled the space.

I looked up. My mouth hung open. *Had April killed Donald? Could you kill a ghost? I mean, they were already dead, weren't they?* I was confused. I placed my hand on the wall to steady myself and rose as the room began to warm. *I knew what I witnessed, but was it real?* I needed time to comprehend what was going on. *Was all of this happening in my head? I really should have listened to the doctors and started seeing a counselor.*

The light returned, first as a spec. It flickered and grew in midair to the size of a baseball. The chill returned and continued to drop again. *He's back! What did he mean when he said his prize? Was I the prize? Was he trying to help me or hurt me?* The last thing I needed was for him to return, considering he might be trying to convince me to take my own life.

The lights flickered and danced; I was mesmerized by their beauty. Something was mysteriously different, the colors and the twinkle and shape. I blushed, knowing this had to be April. The mass grew and took the form of a woman: my girl, my wife, the love of my life, whom I'd missed so much. April appeared. I smiled and sobbed, happy and sad at the same time.

"I can't stay long," April said, frowning. "Don't trust him. He's bad news. He wants to trick you into killing your-self," she urged.

"Is he dead?"

"No."

"I saw you shoot him or something like that." *I wasn't sure what I had seen.*

"I knocked him out, something a friend showed me," April explained.

"I'm confused. Why would he want to hurt or kill me? He's a distant relative." I rubbed my hand on my chin. I grappled with the information April was trying to give me. *It didn't make sense. Why would he want to hurt me? Then, on the other hand, why not? What did he have to lose? I could be with April and Bobby if I took my own life. Why would she not want that? Maybe she had a thing for this old man! Here I go again with the jealousy thing. I was jealous when guys looked at April when she was alive, and what? I was still jealous when she's a ghost.* I concluded that April had my best interest at heart. "Okay, I'm listening,"

"He doesn't care who he torments. He enjoys it. Listen, stay away from Donald, and whatever you do, don't listen to him. Nothing good will come of it."

"I promise I won't listen to him anymore." My gut told me to trust April, and I smiled.

"Bobby and I love you and want you to be happy. We are alright, and we are together." April scrunched her nose and forced a smile.

"I'm sorry. I truly am," I started to say, but April pressed her cold finger to my lips.

"We're not bitter or angry. I must go. I grow tired. Be careful, Bob." She faded and evaporated before me.

"Wait, I have more questions. I love you and Bobby, too!" I sank to the floor and rested my back on the wall. *When would I see her again? Could Bobby show himself? What about Donald Thornhill? When would he return?* I knew what I needed to do.

SIXTEEN

Wednesday, October 16, 1963

Yesterday was a bit of a blur. After my morning encounter with Donald and April, who would blame me for not remembering everything? I spent most of the afternoon remembering the details and processing what I had seen and heard. Tom called a few times to check up on me. It was nice to know someone still cared about me. No one else took the time to call, certainly not April's parents. I guess because they still blamed me for the accident. We all knew it was the teenager's fault, not mine. The thought made my blood boil.

Living in a haunted house or where a spirit resides could be unnerving and devastating. The spirit doing the haunting didn't need to be evil, necessarily. But facing a spirit intent on taking revenge or righting a wrong was daunting. I knew April and Bobby would not hurt me, but the old man could. I also wondered if other spirits resided in my house or the area. I guess only time would tell.

Tom offered me a suggestion, and after a day of thinking about it, I realized some things. Donald Thornhill was not going away. He would be around forever to haunt me. Even if I took my own life, he would still be here. That's assuming I would even become a ghost. But I was too bull-headed to commit suicide. I didn't care how powerful this old fart thought he was. Dead or alive, I would never live an ordinary life again.

As Tom suggested, I called and spent an hour on the phone with Gladys. She could have the answer I needed, but it would come at a price. She said she had to check with some friends and do some research. Heck, I didn't know there were other ladies around who could talk to the spirit world. I guess I'd been living under a rock.

Everything was set. Gladys and Tom were expected to arrive anytime. I scurried about, tidying up the house. I didn't want Gladys to think I was a slob. I was a borderline neat freak if you were to ask Tom. I remembered when I was a slob. Look at me now. I paced back and forth, wondering when they would arrive. It was not like Tom to be late, but he did have a business to run. Or maybe it was Gladys who was running late, and Tom was chomping at the bit to get over here and get this over with.

I walked back and forth, checking the clock on the wall at every third pass. Another minute passed. I heard a noise outside. I darted to the window. A good-sized limb fell from the oak tree some thirty yards from the house. I hadn't even noticed the gloomy day outside. The wind was rustling past at a good pace, and spits of rain dotted the sky.

My nerves were on edge, and rightly so. We were going to call the spirit world and try to end all this nonsense. I caught a glimpse of something out of the corner of my eye.

It darted toward the water, where I noticed a ripple. Maybe it was a beaver or muskrat who entered the water. It didn't matter. So, I focused back on my empty driveway.

I inhaled to calm myself, but that wasn't working. I continued to pace front to back at a more vigorous rate. If I kept this up, I would lose weight. I was not fat, but I could stand to lose a few pounds. I paused, spun, darted to the living room, and pulled the curtains back. Yes, they had arrived.

Gladys was wearing all black, and she carried a large sack. Tom was holding a box under his right arm. I pulled back when a third person climbed out of the car—a much older woman wearing black. I didn't recognize her. She could not have been from around here. I was puzzled but moved to the front door to let them enter.

"Good to see you, Tom," I said as he passed to my right. "Thank you, Gladys, for coming." I nodded and smiled. "Hello, I'm Bob," I said with an outstretched hand toward the older woman. She walked past me, not saying a word. I closed the door behind them.

"We have work to do, Bob," Gladys said and motioned me to have a seat. I did as instructed and placed my rump on the couch. Tom put the box in the center of the table and sat next to me.

"Who's the other lady?" I asked. Tom raised his finger to his lips to silence me.

"Quiet, please." She approached and placed a necklace around my neck, then another one around Tom's neck. I wrapped my hand around it, feeling the odd shape. I pulled it up to my eyes. It was some sort of carved stone that looked like an odd-shaped bull with horns. I guess this was going to protect us. My necklace matched Tom's, and

I noticed both women wore the same odd-shaped stone around their necks. *I felt safer already.*

Gladys and the other woman moved about with ease—lighting and placing candles about the house and closing blinds and curtains. The two ladies pushed my coffee table to one side, clearing the room. The older woman pulled a large jar of salt from her bag and drew a big circle of salt in the middle of the floor. They appeared to have done this before.

I watched as the salt formed a ring and thought about how much of a mess this was going to be to clean up. *I would have to borrow Tom's vacuum from the store to get all the salt out of the carpet.* I thought back to a remark Gladys had made before. *Did the salt protect us from spirits?* Gladys pulled a bag of incense from the box and placed incense around the room. The fragrance was sure to burn my nose.

I sat silently on the couch and watched the two ladies, or should I call them witches, work their magic. They paused, glanced at each other, and slowly turned to Tom and me. The older woman motioned for us to stand. She extended her hand. I didn't want to upset anyone, so I quickly placed my hand in hers. Her skin was clammy. *Was she nervous?* That didn't sit well with me. *If she was unsure, then why should I feel good about what was going to happen?*

She joined Tom on the other side, and we each took hold of one of Gladys's hands. I was baffled, not knowing how to react or what to do. I was hoping they would offer some sort of guidance. *All I knew was that I wanted to get this over with and hoped for success.* Over the past year, I have learned to trust Gladys. She was the real deal. The woman whose name I didn't know wouldn't be here unless Gladys trusted her, and that was good enough for me.

Gladys started to mumble something; I believed it was a chant of some sort. It sounded like "Om," but I was not sure. It was just a steady hum, "Om." It started softly and grew. I held on tightly and closed my eyes. I sure hoped this necklace and the salt worked.

The older woman started to hum the same tune, "Om." *Were we supposed to join them?* I was a little annoyed at not receiving any instructions. I tried to keep my thoughts to myself because Gladys had a way of knowing what my thoughts were.

I heard Tom start to say, "Om." I took that as my cue to join them. I started softly, then increased the volume as they did.

Our voices grew louder. I opened one eye. The house was smoky like a fog had rolled in. I glanced left and right to ensure there wasn't a large fire in my house. *We were safe for the moment.*

The older woman stopped, and Gladys and Tom continued, so I followed in tow and continued to say, "Om." I squinted with one eye and caught a glimpse of her opening a small book.

"Rid this home," she began to read. One arm held the small book, and the other stretched at her side, with her hand wide open as if praying. "Rid this home of all spirits, good and bad." She repeated this phrase until I was tired of hearing her say it. "Rid this home of all spirits, good, bad, and evil," she read. *Well, that was different.* I smiled.

"Rid this home and valley of all spirits, good, bad, and evil," she added.

Well, now we were going to banish them from the valley? That's cool. I wondered what kind of power she contained.

"Rid this home and valley of all spirits, good, bad, and evil." She thrust her hand forward. She repeated this process over and over. Her voice grew louder every time she recited the verse.

I noticed something in her hand. *Did she have holy water? Or was it some potion she and Gladys cooked up?* My mind raced. Something felt off-kilter.

"Rid this home and valley of all spirits, good, bad, and evil," she hollered, repeating the process, and she continued to fling her hand forward in a different direction each time.

We continued to chant, "Om." I was getting the hang of it now.

I'd lost track of time. My throat grew sore, and I could really use a glass of water. I was sure I wasn't the only one who felt this way. The old lady lowered her voice. *Good, maybe she wanted a drink, too.* She paused, with both hands stretched toward the ceiling. "Sleep, my children, until you are called to wake," she whispered several times.

Gladys and Tom both stopped chanting, so I did the same. I felt Gladys and the old lady release my hand in unison. I opened my eyes wide; it was funny how the smoke cleared so quickly. I glanced about the house. The day seemed brighter. A peaceful feeling flooded me. I smiled. I felt calm and relaxed for the first time in two years.

Gladys and the old woman went about their business, gathering the incense and half-burned candles.

"Bob, I'll stick around if you can give me a ride home," Tom asked.

"Um, sure, not a problem," I said. I was glad Tom was going to hang out for a little while. It would give us a chance to chat.

The ladies packed things up, not asking for any help. They even brushed as much salt as they could back into the glass jar and spun the lid closed. The older woman paused before me and smiled. Then, she gave a nod and proceeded to the car.

Gladys approached. "Everything is going to be fine, dear. You are safe now," she said. She gave me a quaint smile and a pat on the shoulder before heading out the door.

They were halfway out the door before I thought about my manners. "Thank you. Oh, thank you both," I said. I hoped they could hear me.

I turned to face Tom. "What did she mean I was *safe now*?"

"Sit." Tom pointed to the couch. "While I'm up, do you have any Pepsi?" He opened the refrigerator door. "Yes." He pulled out two bottles, and I heard them opening. Tom handed me a bottle, and I quickly pushed the bottle to my lips, taking a gulp.

"Dry mouth?" Tom asked.

"Just a little."

"You asked what Mom meant when she said you're safe now."

"Yes, are they gone?"

"Not exactly. You have to find out what is keeping their spirits from crossing over. Then, you must solve it so they can move on. No, Mom and her friend performed a sleep charm. So now the spirit world can rest until someone opens the portal," Tom said.

"How do you open the portal or wake them up?" I asked.

"You would need to tell their story, reminisce in the past. Or find their remains. Something like that, at least that is what Mom said," Tom replied.

"I guess there are many ways to open the window?" I asked.

"You could say that."

"What about April and Bobby?"

Tom frowned. "Sorry, man. Resting."

I didn't know how to respond. *No more sounds, games, or baseball gloves? No food smells coming from the kitchen? No voices? No April? This was going to hurt. It had taken time to get used to the spirits; now they were gone. Maybe April and Bobby would still be around. Time would tell.*

SEVENTEEN

Thursday, September 17, 1964

It's funny how time could slip away from us. One minute, it's summer, and in the blink of an eye, it's fall, and the leaves were changing on the trees. Here it was, approaching the third anniversary of the passing of my wife and child. *Where did the time go?*

I hadn't seen or heard from Bobby or April since last October. I wasn't sure if she was trying to keep her distance. Maybe Bobby's and her presence made the old man want to visit me. Or maybe Tom and Gladys were right. They were resting, or sleeping, whatever you wanted to call it. I guess the spell worked. It's not easy being alone. I'd never felt this much pain. I had to say, it was nice to see them from time to time. Now I sat alone, staring at these four walls. These past eleven months had been brutal.

I'd had too much time to think. It made me wonder how time worked in the spirit world. *Did the time work the same? Was it slower or faster? Did spirits even care about time? Did they watch the world and the people they cared about come and go? When they were resting, what happened to their souls? What did it mean to be sleeping? Did they have a safe hiding place?*

I needed to get my mind off these weird thoughts and focus on the real world and the living. I hadn't seen Tom or Gladys for a few weeks now. They knew I was struggling with the emptiness. Tom and Gladys would invite me over for dinner at least once a month. I enjoyed their company. I was shocked when Tom invited me to go away for the weekend. Maybe that was the break I needed—time away from this house.

Tom had been ranting about the World's Fair that was happening in New York. He wanted to go so badly, and after weeks of Tom hounding me, I broke down and finally gave in. We were taking a long weekend to go to New York. The time away would do me good, but it also made me suspicious about what would happen here at the house. I didn't want any of the local boys trespassing on my property. Every time I turned around, I saw one of those kids lurking or spying from the woods. Tom thought I was going stir-crazy, but I knew what I'd seen: those boys that I didn't trust. My blood boiled every time I thought about it.

Lately, all Tom talked about was the Ford Mustang, some new car that was coming out; it would be all the rage. The vehicle of the future, it's not something my dealership would carry. It would be our competitor, so if I liked the car, I could not buy one. I'd stick with my 1961 Plymouth Belvedere. It had a 318 Hemi engine and hummed like a beast. I couldn't stop Tom from buying a Mustang if he wanted one. I would not even try. That wouldn't be right. The only place to see them was at the World's Fair. A hard top and a convertible would be released in 1965. The car looked sharp from the pictures Tom showed me in the magazines. But we had to see for ourselves. There was nothing like sitting behind the wheel of a power car.

Tom had done his homework. He mapped out our trip and even picked a nice KOA campground about thirty minutes from the New York fairgrounds. That was fine with me. I was never comfortable staying in a hotel, not knowing who'd slept on the bed the day before and whether they'd cleaned the sheets. I'd snuggle up in my sleeping bag any time. It's only for a few nights. The weather would be perfect, mid-seventies in the day and low sixties at night. That would make for perfect sleeping weather. We packed my family-size tent in the trunk, along with our sleeping bags, camp stove, and a few bags of canned food. It was nothing fancy, but it was fine for a couple of country boys like Tom and me.

Once the car was packed, we swung by the General Store and topped off the tank. *I hadn't taken a vacation for as long as I could remember. I always talked about taking April and Bobby to Niagara Falls. It's one more thing I never got around to—shame on me.*

"Are you done?" Tom asked.

"Aw, yeah." I snapped out of my daze, hung up the handle, put the gas cap back on the car, and closed the license plate.

Bobby would have wanted to tag along with us if he were still alive. He would have been thirteen. I was sure April would have said yes. We could have called it a guy's trip. If he were anything like me, he would have loved cars. Just the thought sent a shiver down my spine. I walked around and climbed into the driver's seat. Then the car roared to life.

"You, okay?" Tom looked concerned.

"I'm fine." I nodded.

"Bobby or April?"

I looked at Tom for a moment before I answered. "I didn't hear or see anything if that's what you mean. I thought about how Bobby would have enjoyed a trip like this. The three of us."

"Keep them close to your heart," Tom said as he tapped his chest.

It's not the conversation I intended to have while I was driving. But I did trust Tom enough to share almost everything with him. "There are days when I miss them more than others. The weekends are the toughest. I miss when they were around—waking in the kitchen, smelling the bacon, and hearing them laugh. It felt so real. The smell would grow stronger as I made my way down the hallway. Bobby and April would be sitting at the table having breakfast. After a few moments, they would evaporate into thin air. How I long for them."

"I believe you; I told you before. Mom talks to spirits, and she told me Bobby and April are still in your home, only resting," Tom said in a comforting tone.

"I'm still a skeptic, even though I've seen things I can't explain. It doesn't mean it's not in my head." I grimaced. "I wish I would have done more with Bobby. Gosh, what I wouldn't give to have had more time with both of them."

"I understand, but you can't second guess your life. Live each day as if it's your last." Tom paused to reflect. "With that being said, let's focus on what we will see at the

World's Fair. Like my new Mustang." Tom cheered and smiled, and I pushed the gas pedal to the floor.

We drove for several hours, stopping once for gas and a quick potty break. We pulled into the KOA campground and followed the instructions on where to find our little spot of land to pitch our tent. We hustled about setting up the tent first. It was an excellent ten-by-ten structure, offering plenty of room for our gear and sleeping bags. I had worked up a sweat and appetite. Tom stepped outside, put some charcoal on the grill, sprayed lighter fluid on top, and tossed a match. The fire blazed to life. I could see the yellow ball of flames from inside the tent. I stepped out to join Tom and handed him a Pepsi from the cooler and two hamburger patties for the grill. Dinner was ready in no time. We polished off our food and decided to swing by the Fair to see what all the fuss was about. After cleaning up, Tom agreed to drive, and I was okay with that since I had been behind the wheel the last five hours on the curvy roads, up and down the back hills of the Pennsylvania mountains. *Tom could deal with the city traffic and try to find a parking place. I had my motives*!

The traffic was not as bad as I expected it would be. Once we found a parking spot, we walked to the entrance and paid our two-dollar admission fee. We found a bench, pulled out the map they gave us, and studied the layout of the Fairgrounds. We started our stroll through the Sinclair Dinoland exhibit—lifesize replicas from prehistoric times. Personally, I thought the T-rex would have been taller. I swung into one of the souvenir stands and picked up a plastic dinosaur for Bobby. Tom looked on but never said a word. He was more than my cousin. He was my best friend and understood everything. I just wanted to get my little man something special in case he came back to visit. Something caught my attention. Okay, it was someone. I tossed the money on the counter and started to jog. Tom jerked me back. "Where are you going?"

"I don't know," I huffed. I then pointed toward the tall, thin blonde wearing a lovely pink dress. She held hands with a boy about fifty feet in front of us. The boy appeared to be about the same age as Bobby.

"That's not April and Bobby," Tom said sternly.

"I would recognize her anywhere." I frowned. I just had a feeling. I shoved Tom and started to jog after the woman and child. I wanted to see if I was right. *Maybe April's parents moved her to New York and paid the doctor and hospital to lie to me so April could live a better life than I could provide.* The woman and her son turned to look at the stegosaurus. The armor plates on its back were massive. She glanced in my direction; it was clear this was not April, and that was not Bobby. I stopped dead in my tracks as Tom caught up to me.

"Sorry," I said to Tom. "I'm not sure what I was thinking." I felt foolish. I glanced at the lady again. She stared at me momentarily, probably thinking I was some sort of weirdo.

"Hey, don't worry about it. Now let's find my Mustang."

We left Dinoland and continued onward past the giant U.S. Royal Tires exhibit. I glanced back a time or two to ensure her looks hadn't changed. I was not sure how that could happen, but half the things in my life were unexplainable—like this giant tire I was looking at. It stood taller than the T-Rex.

Maybe Tom should stock these tires at the store. My nostrils flared as I caught a whiff of some Coney hot dogs on the grill. We stepped over, and they looked delicious;

there's nothing better than a New York style Coney Island chili cheese dog. "Mmm, Mmm." I smiled. Even though we had already eaten, Tom and I decided to tackle the giant twelve-inch hotdogs. I wanted to eat another one, but my stomach felt bloated.

We walked at a slower pace, waiting for our food to digest. Darkness fell, and slowly, all one hundred forty exhibits closed for the day. The Mustang would have to wait for tomorrow.

The next day, we took in as many sites as possible. The Skyride and new Disney Monorail made it easy to get from one side of the park to the other. Tom finally got a chance to sit behind the wheel of what would become his new Ford Mustang. I must admit, the car was sharp. But my personal favorite was the new GM-X Stiletto concept car. "The Automobile of the Future," the sign read. Its black hood with bright cherry-red car paint resembled a spaceship more than a car. "New Jet-Age Design," the banner read. Its sleek design was something I could see myself driving one day, maybe when I retired.

We lollygagged about the Flags of Nations exhibit and were in awe of the giant metal sphere shaped like planet Earth. Yes, it was taller than the T-Rex, too. Planet Earth was surrounded by water and had an excellent fountain display.

Disneyland had four exhibits at the Fair, all sponsored by Pepsi and UNICEF. They debuted "It's a Small World," a new ride coming to their California theme park. I was mesmerized by the Abraham Lincoln Audio-Animatronic statue. He moved and talked. Gosh, April and Bobby would have loved this place. The spaceships and rockets were unique, taller than I ever imagined, and taller than the T-Rex. This place reminded me of one of the Saturday morning cartoons, *The Jetsons*. I guess everything was pointing to space travel in the future. Even NASA was talking about putting a man on the moon. I hoped I would live long enough to see it. It was interesting to see where technology would take the human race.

Our weekend getaway was over in a flash. We packed up first thing Monday morning and were on the road as the sun rose. With a bit of luck, we would be home around noon. That would give Tom a chance to open the store and me a chance to relax a little before going back to work tomorrow. The first thing I wanted to do when I got home was put the dinosaur on Bobby's dresser.

EIGHTEEN

Friday, June 6, 1975

The years passed. I did my best to keep everyone away from my house except Tom and Gladys. But I saw less of Gladys in the past few years due to her age. I was getting older too and had become more of a recluse. I was not too fond of it when the local boys floated past on the water. I wanted to figure out how to keep them out, but it would be tricky. I couldn't block the creek. That could flood my land, and I already had issues when we would get too much rain. I even thought about stretching rope across the creek. Maybe that would knock them off their makeshift rafts.

I hadn't seen or heard from April or Bobby in over ten years. I had to admit, I missed them both being around. But, deep inside, I knew they were still with me. I never saw Donald again, or any other ghost for that matter. Not since Gladys and the other woman had put them to sleep. I guess the spell really worked. But I made sure to clean Bobby's room once a month, placing everything back in the same place — even the dinosaur.

I heard a car door slam outside. I walked over to the couch and pulled the curtain back. Just as I thought, Tom was here. "It's open," I yelled.

"Hey Bob, what's cooking?" Tom asked as he strolled into the room.

"I'm having bacon and eggs." I gazed at the plate of food in my hands.

"Ah, brinner, I love doing that."

"Brinner?" I was curious.

"Yeah, breakfast for dinner. Brinner," Tom said and laughed at his joke.

I shook my head. Tom and his funny ways. Brinner. *That was clever*. "Do you want some?" I asked.

"No, I'm good, but thanks." Tom smiled and placed a box on the floor.

I stared at the large cardboard box. "Whatcha got there?" I pointed. I sat up straight when the box moved. "Tom?"

Tom pushed the box closer to me. "I found this little fellow around the back of the store. He needs a good home." Tom hoisted a little, brown-colored puppy out and held him high for me to see.

"No, no pets. I can't take care of a dog," I snarled at Tom. The puppy was cute and shot me a sad look.

"Ah, come on, he needs a home," Tom pleaded. "And you need a friend."

"I have a friend, and right now, he's annoying me," I said with a sidelong stare.

Tom frowned. "Really, just look at this little fellow. He needs you." Tom was almost begging. That was the last thing I needed… to watch a grown man beg.

Over the past twelve years, Tom had tried to fix me up on dates. *If Tom was such a romantic, why didn't he have a girlfriend?* He always said he was a player. I always told him you have to date to be a player.

Even the ladies at work have tried to set me up with dates. I chuckled inside. *I was better off alone. I knew that, and Tom knew that. So why would he give me a puppy?* He was cute as he jumped out of Tom's hands into my lap. "He's a playful little guy." I smiled.

"I knew you would love him," Tom said.

"But I don't have any dog food." I pushed the puppy toward Tom, who ignored me. I was looking for excuses. He reached into the box and pulled out a small bag of puppy food. He stood and went to the kitchen and grabbed two cereal bowls. I watched as he filled one with water, then ripped the bag open, and poured food into the other bowl. The little pup bolted for the food and lapped it up quickly. He licked a little from the water bowl, bounced back into my lap, and snuggled. I stroked his soft fur, and my heart warmed. *How could I turn my back on a helpless animal? He's going to need a name.*

"Give him about a quarter cup twice daily," Tom said. "He'll eat more as he gets older.

Something caught the little guy's attention. He jumped out of my lap and started exploring his new surroundings, sniffing this and that as he worked his way around the living room. *They said cats and dogs have heightened senses. I wondered if he would know when Bobby and April were present or if he could tell where they were resting. I knew it'd been almost fourteen years since the accident. Heck, maybe the little guy could alert me when someone was on my property. Then, no one would sneak onto my land again without me knowing. This dog was going to work out well.*

"Earth to Bob," Tom snapped.

"Sorry, I'm trying to think of a good name for this lucky fellow," I lied about my thoughts, then scooped up the last bite of my "Brinner."

"Great, I knew you would love him, and thank you for saving his life," Tom added.

"Maybe I'll call him Brinner," I joked. I wasn't even sure what kind of a dog he was, more like a mutt, a mix of everything. But he had the coolest-looking eyes. "Bright Eye? No. Oh, I got it, Storm Chaser? No, that doesn't work. Yes. I got it!" I yelled.

"You got what?"

"Tom, meet Spy," I said and pointed at the pup while he sniffed my slippers.

Tom smiled and nodded. "Spy? Really? I'm not fond of it, but it will work."

"Can you do better?" I asked.

"I was thinking Mustang," Bob said and gave a little laugh.

"Of course, you were. Okay, how about Duke?" I said, spreading my hands.

"No, I got it." Tom gleamed. "Tank."

I looked down at my feet and made eye contact with the puppy. There was something about his build; I could tell he was built, and the name would fit perfectly. "Okay, Tom, meet Tank."

Tom walked over and rubbed the little guy's back. "Hi Tank, I told you I would find you a good home. I know you will love it here."

Tom left shortly after that, leaving the two of us to get to know one another. Tank was so playful. I found a small rubber ball in Bobby's room and tossed it repeatedly while Tank retrieved it, bringing it back to me each time. He was a natural ball player.

It was dark out, and I grew tired from playing with Tank. The little guy had more energy than I did. Everywhere I went, he was under my feet. I felt like I had a new shadow, and I loved it. I felt like I had a purpose again. Once again, I owed Tom a big thank you.

I grabbed a blanket from the closet, folded it, and placed it in the corner of the room for Tank to sleep on. I sat him down and wished him a good night's sleep. I turned and crawled under the sheet. Tank had other plans. I felt him pounce on the bed and snuggle at my side. I smiled and laid my head on the pillow.

My eyes sprang open. I jolted forward. The moonlight shining through a crack in the curtains cast an eerie feeling over the room. A shiver raced down my spine. The wind howled; the trees swayed from side to side. *They didn't mention a storm on the nightly news.* Something was wrong. I could feel it but had no clue what it could be. The wind roared past. A flash of lightning lit up the room. Everything went dark. *The clouds must be blocking the moon. It was too early for a summer storm in Pennsylvania.* Tank whimpered. I scooped him up and comforted him in my arms. His little heart raced, and he shivered. I waited for the roar of thunder, but it never came.

The moonlight lit up the room, and the wind ended as quickly as it had come. I forced myself out of bed and looked out the window. Another chill ran down my spine. *No sound—crickets, owls, nothing. I found that a little odd. No movement either.* The ripples from the stream twinkled and slowly rolled past as the moonlight cast its reflection.

A woman wearing a long white dress stood next to the shoreline. *April? She was young, and I could tell this was not April.* I blinked, and she was gone. *Okay, now my mind was playing tricks on me.* I glanced from side to side as far as I could see but found nothing. *I must be seeing things. Was I dreaming this?* I made my way back to bed. I pulled the cover to my neck. Tank snuggled at my feet. I closed my eyes and smiled.

NINETEEN

Saturday, June 7, 1975

After a restless night of sleep, something wet forced my eyes open. I wasn't used to having a dog in my bed. *Oh, I know. I was sure he needed to use the bathroom.* I sprang to my feet, slipped my slippers on, and darted for the door. Tank scampered behind. Nudging it open, Tank sprang to the porch, then to the lawn. I smiled. *I think he was feeling a bit relieved.*

He quietly did his business and ran back to the door. *He must be hungry.* I let him pass and watched as he sprinted for his bowl. I grabbed the puppy food Tom had left me, scooped a quarter cup as instructed, and poured it into the bowl. I noticed he had plenty of water. Tank gobbled every piece of food. I opened the hall closet and grabbed a bath towel. With Tank on my heels, I folded it and spread it out in a circular shape so Tank had a place to sleep. I noticed April's large rubber bathmat on the bathroom floor. I grabbed that and put it next to the entryway door. Then, I scooped up a stack of newspapers and spread them over the bathmat, giving Tank a place to go if I forgot to let him out.

I needed to make a list of things I would need for Tank. I picked up my scratch pad and ink pen, then took my spot at the kitchen table. My thoughts raced to the events of last night. *A five-minute storm but no rain? Winds and lightning yet no thunder? How bazaar! I had never seen anything like that in all my years. Oh, wait, what about the woman wearing the white dress? Who was she? What was she doing at my house? Why was she standing outside next to the water's edge in that weather?* I lunged from my chair. An eeriness flooded me when a knock came at the front door. A shiver ran down my spine. I had a terrible feeling about this.

I slowly opened the door. Tom stood before me. He looked rough, like he hadn't slept in days. "Are you alright?" I asked.

Tom walked past me, stopping in the middle of the room. He then turned to face me. "No, I don't know," Tom said. He looked puzzled. He paced back and forth and fumbled in his pocket.

"Relax, have a seat. I pulled out a chair."

"Thanks," Tom said and trembled.

"Were you robbed? Did Jimmy steal something from you?" My tone was nasty. *I didn't trust him or the Malone boys, and especially the Parker kids. Well, the older Parker girl seemed nice and had some manners.*

"No, you know I trust him. He's a good kid," Tom said with a half-smile. "You're making me forget why I stopped over. Oh, yes. Did, ah, something happen last night?" Tom asked. *Now, I was the one who was puzzled.*

"What do you mean?" I queried. *Had Tom experienced the same storm as I? Of course, he did. I was sure half the county had woken up in the middle of the night.*

"Well…" Tom hesitated. "How did you sleep last night? With the new puppy and all?"

"Everything was fine until the storm arrived," I said. "Then…" I decided to shut my mouth about the woman in the dress.

"Okay." Tom showed his pearly whites like some crazy person waving his finger at me. "Yes, me too. But this morning, after I opened the store and the customers started rolling in, things got weird."

"Weird, how?"

"Well, John Stapleton stopped to fill up his car. I asked if he lost power last night, and he didn't have a clue. He said he must have slept through the storm," Tom said and continued. "It wasn't just him—the Doc, Mr. Parker, Mr. Hanson, Mrs. Braden, and several others. No storm," Tom said, leaving me to wonder, *Did I even hear and see what I thought last night?*

"Is Jimmy watching the store this morning?" I asked.

"No, he's camping. It's the first weekend of summer vacation. I guess it's a new tradition."

"Who's running the store?" I asked, more puzzled now than before. Tom doesn't like to close on Saturday.

"Listen, something happened last night. So far, you and I are the only ones who heard or saw the storm," he said, a hint of desperation in his voice.

"What are you saying, Tom?" I turned pale.

We both jumped when the phone rang. I glanced at the kitchen wall where the phone hung. It rang again. "Are you going to answer it?" Tom asked.

I gritted my teeth and walked slowly toward the phone. It rang a third time. "Answer the phone!" Tom yelled at me. "I think it's Mom."

I shrugged, extended my hand, grabbed the receiver, and placed it to my ear. "Good morning, Bob. I hope I didn't wake you," Gladys said.

"No, I've been up for a little bit. How are you doing, Gladys?"

Tom was growing impatient, his stare burning through me like a light beam. "It's your mother," I mouthed the words. "How did you know?"

"That's not good," Tom said and frowned as he shook his head.

"Sorry, Gladys, I was just telling Tom it was you on the phone," I said.

"I'm sure he knew it was me," Gladys said. "I'm glad you are both together. I will only have to say this once. Someone woke them." The phone went silent.

I thought about her statement. "Woke who?" I questioned.

"I think you know what I'm talking about, Bob."

"No, I don't know what you are talking about."

"Tell Tom to come closer to the phone," Gladys said, and I did as instructed.

I motioned with my hand, and Tom moved to my side. We each placed an ear to the phone to hear what Gladys was about to tell us.

"Are you both here?"

"Yes," we said in unison.

"Good. Did you both feel the storm last night?"

"Yes," we both said, slightly off this time.

"It was not a rain or thunderstorm, not at all. It was a spiritual rising. Someone awakened the spirit world. Only the three of us felt it because we were there when the spell was cast."

"What are you talking about? How is that possible? You said they were asleep," I said, more harshly than I meant.

"I knew it," Tom whispered. "I had this feeling when I woke this morning."

"You have a gift, my son. It's been passed to you. Now, we need to work on your development. But we have a bigger issue now." Gladys paused.

"I still don't understand," I said.

"Dear boy, let me explain. I'm sure you remember when my friend and I visited your house eleven years ago. We performed a witch's sleeping charm to rest the spirit world," Gladys said.

"I remember that night." That was the first time Gladys had referred to herself as a witch.

"My friend and I put the spirit world to rest. I also told you they could be awakened if someone wanted to. Have you been talking to anyone about April, Bobby, and Mr. Thornhill?"

"No, not at all," I said quietly.

"Well, someone woke them, maybe by accident," Gladys said.

"Who would do such a thing?" I said, with a slightly panicked tone in my voice. "So, what do we do now?" I said as my anxiety soared to new heights.

"I don't have all the answers, Bob," Gladys said.

"Well, can you hurry over and put them back to sleep?"

"I wish it were that easy. Unfortunately, it's not."

"Why not?!" I yelled. "Sorry, I didn't mean to yell. I'm…
I'm nervous, and I don't want to face Mr. Thornhill again.
He scares me."

"Do you remember Mabel?"

"Who?" I asked.

"Mabel was the witch who came with me to your house.
She was my equal, and together, we could perform the spell
required to put the spirit world to rest. But she passed away
a few years ago, and I know no other equal," Gladys said.
I detected a sad tone in her voice.

"I'm sorry about Mabel." *Wow, eleven years, and I
finally found out her name was Mabel. Why didn't she tell
me that day? On the other hand, I did feel bad for Gladys.
She never really had many friends. I guess it was hard
making friends when you were a witch.*

"Thank you, Bob."

"So, what do we do now?" Tom asked.

"There's not much we can do. Let's see what happens over the next few days and weeks, and we will try to
devise a plan.

"I can learn the spell and do it with you," Tom said as
he bounced on the balls of his feet.

"I said you have a gift, but it would take years to perfect
it. But we can start with a few basic charms and enchant-
ments," Gladys said.

"I'm ready, Mom,"

"We can talk about that more in detail tonight. For now,
boys, be safe and open your eyes to anything suspicious.
Oh, one more thing… Do you still have the pendant neck-
laces I gave you? You should wear them," Gladys said, followed by a click and a ringtone.

Just like that, she had hung up. Tom quickly exited because it was Saturday, and that was a busy day for him. I sat on the couch and wondered about Tank and my safety.

TWENTY

Saturday Afternoon, June 7, 1975

Shortly after Tom left, I decided to take Tank out for a walk around the grounds. He was a curious little fellow, stopping to sniff every tree and spread his scent. He knew this was his house and yard. Dogs were intelligent like that. He sprinted off toward one of the larger trees at the edge of my property, and I watched as the squirrel scurried up the side and out of danger. Tank barked and barked and danced around the base until I arrived. He refused to leave, so I finally had to pick him up and carry him back to the house.

I pushed the door open to the smell of bacon. Tank's nose shot to attention, and he searched for the source of that beautiful aroma. I glanced right and left, but there was no sign of April, Bobby, or that mean old man. I walked to Bobby's room, Tank on my heels. I opened the door— nothing out of place here. I returned to the kitchen, opened the refrigerator, and checked the freezer section. I then shuffled a few things around, disappointed that I didn't have any bacon.

That meant one thing. I went to the bedroom, grabbed my wallet and keys, scooped Tank up with one arm, and closed the door behind me. I needed bacon, and if my memory served me correctly, Tom sold that at the General Store. It was only a mile or so down the road, and I didn't feel like driving all the way into town.

I pulled in, parking my gray 1961 Plymouth on the side. Tank's little paws were on the edge of the door, and he stared out the window at the trees. I looked up, noticing all the crows perched on the branches. *I didn't know if I had ever seen that many crows in one place before.* I rolled the window down a crack and opened the door, closing it behind me. I instructed Tank to stay put because I would be right back. *It's not like he would open the door or anything like that. This was for his safety. I didn't want any of the crows trying to take him.* The bells chimed when I opened the door. Tom was nowhere in sight, but I knew he was there because his Mustang was parked in the rear of the store. I moseyed to the freezer, opened the door, and, yes, I was in luck. Tom had bacon, and I grabbed a pack and a loaf of bread, not knowing how fresh mine was at the house. I also decided to pick up a gallon of milk. I set the items on the counter. "Tom," I hollered. I heard shuffling sounds coming from his office, and then the door opened.

Tom didn't say a word. He rang the groceries up and pulled a brown paper bag from under the counter. I watched as he stuffed the items into the bag. "Are you alright, Tom?" I asked, my voice stern. He shook his head a little and gazed at me with a blank stare. He appeared to be lost. "Are you okay, Tom?" I asked again. Tom didn't move. His eyes were dark-colored, almost black. "Tom!" I hollered.

His eyes blinked, and the darkness faded. "Yes," he said slowly. He appeared puzzled. "How long have you been standing there?"

"Long enough to know something is wrong with you."

"That's weird. I don't remember the last few things I did," Tom said, looking back and forth.

"Maybe it's from the lack of sleep last night," I added, handing Tom a ten-dollar bill.

Tom counted my change and placed it onto the counter. "Are you going to be alright?"

"I'm fine now. I'm glad you stopped in," Tom said.

"Are you sure? I can hang around for a bit," I said.

"I'm good," Tom said, giving me his usual smile.

My timing was perfect. What was happening with Tom concerned me, but he was doing well now. The bells at the pump rang out. Tom looked outside; he had a gas customer, and I walked out behind him as he made his way to the car's rear. I gave a quick wave, opened the door, and placed the bag onto the floorboards.

Tank jumped up on my lap to get a better view outside. I noticed many of the branches were empty. Only two large crows remained. I had to do a double take. Yes, they were crows, but they were the size of bald eagles. I was glad I didn't let Tank follow me inside. One of those birds could have carried Tank away.

I revved up the engine and headed for the house. I drove slowly so Tank could look at the creek and the forest surrounding our home. I noticed the tall brush on both sides of the driveway. Many of those bushes have grown a lot in the past few years. I pulled in and parked along the side of the house. I let Tank out to do his business and quickly went inside to get my brunch cooking. After the strange smell of bacon, I had a craving for it. I ran hot water over the pack to thaw it. I grabbed a few eggs, prepped the toast in the toaster, and placed the large skillet onto the stove. I cranked up the gas and waited.

Moments later, I turned the water off, peeled the bacon strips apart, and carefully laid them in the frying pan. I loved the sizzling sound the bacon made as it was frying. The smell quickly filled the house. I finished a few pieces, placing them onto a paper towel to absorb the grease. I put more strips into the pan. I grabbed a slice of bacon and shoved it into my mouth. "Mmm," I said. *There was nothing better than freshly cooked bacon.*

I heard a dog barking in the distance. Oh shoot, I left Tank outside. He probably smelled the bacon and wanted a piece for himself. I strolled to the door, and Tank was not on the porch. I shoved the door open and heard Tank. I quickly ran to the side of the house and spotted the little fellow next to the creek. Maybe he spotted something. This could be dangerous if he had encountered a muskrat or beaver. I noticed a group of boys floating past the house on large Styrofoam rafts. This was the same group of characters I chased out of here last year. I remembered because I was making spaghetti, and I noticed them on the creek. *They were making an awful racket, playing, and carrying on like they didn't have a care in the world. I raced outside, holding the large wooden spoon covered in sauce. One of them laughed at me, and I threw the spoon at him. It wasn't even close. They laughed and yelled not-so-nice things at me. One of them called me a dork as they swam out of sight.*

When I got back inside the house, I felt stupid. That was my last wooden spoon; after that, I had to use a metal spoon that scratched the Teflon frying pan to heat the sauce. Not to mention, I had to buy another wooden spoon the next time I was in town. What a waste of money. Sometimes, I wish I thought before I reacted.

I took a few steps toward the creek. The boys slid into the water, trying to hide behind their rafts, but I could still see them. Tank had done his job. He caught these troublemakers on my property. I knew a dog who would be rewarded with a slice of bacon. "You boys better be gone before I get back, or there's gonna be trouble!" I yelled, turning toward the house. I recognized the Malone brothers, Buck and Johnny, and the Parker boy. Now, he was a sneaky character if I ever spotted one. Then there was Jimmy Brooker, who helped Tom around the store. I wasn't sure of the other boys' names, but I had seen them around a time or two. I tossed the screen door open and sprinted to my bedroom. I opened the closet and grabbed my shotgun. I darted to the dresser and opened a box of buckshot shells. Placing two in the chamber and a few extra rounds in my pocket, I dashed down the hallway and out onto the porch. I was sprinting toward the water's edge. The boys were close to the edge of my property line. I needed to send a message, one they would understand. I was done playing. I just wanted to scare the crap out of them, so I pointed the gun up into the air in the opposite direction of the kids and pulled the trigger.

I heard them screaming and yelling. I laughed on the inside, grabbed two more buckshot shells, and loaded them to fire another warning shot. I fired another round as the boys scrambled out of sight. I laughed and smiled some more. I turned to thank Tank for pointing them out. I noticed the little guy was crouched down in the grass. Ah, the poor boy was scared. "Hey Tank, I'm sorry. I didn't mean to scare you. That must have been loud on your little ears." I scooped him up in my left arm while I balanced the rifle in the other. *That reminded me…I had better stop at the motorcycle shop and complain about the Styrofoam piled out back of their store.* The store was careless; the new bikes were packed in Styrofoam, and they just tossed it all in the rear of the store.

I pushed the door open to a pungent smell of burnt bacon. "Crap, you boys are going to pay for this," I said, knowing they couldn't hear me, but it didn't mean I couldn't let out my frustration. I moved the frying pan to a different burner, then leaned over the kitchen sink to open the window and let in some fresh air. I waved my hands around like a lunatic trying to clear the smoke. I tossed the burnt bacon in Tank's food bowl, and he darted over, quickly turned up his nose, and walked away. *An intelligent dog. I wouldn't eat that either.* I walked to the family room and opened the large window. I hoped this would create a crosswind and clear the house sooner. From the looks of things, I would say it was working.

I knelt, rubbed Tank's head and back, and thanked him for telling me the boys were trespassing. He pushed into me to show me his love. Just for that, he would get a second piece of bacon.

I hoped the boys thought I was crazy for firing my gun. *Crap, I had done it again. It never occurred to me that I was breaking the law. What if they told their parents to come here with the local rent-a-cop?* I felt a little uneasy with my actions. My mind kicked into overdrive. *Well, if they did, I'd call in a favor to Tom. He and the fuzz had a good relationship.*

The house was clearing out rather quickly, but I knew the smell would be around for a while. I flipped the latch on the screen door so Tank couldn't get out. I tossed a few more strips of raw bacon into the pan, added the eggs, and pushed the bread down into the toaster. "There's nothing better than this, Tank." Breakfast for lunch, or brunch, as the younger folks called it. It also worked for dinner, or brinner, as Tom called it.

I placed the first strip of bacon on the paper towel to absorb the grease. Then, I tossed it in Tank's bowl as a reward for spotting those kids. I watched him pig out. Gosh, for a little fellow, he scarfed that down quickly. I scooped up the eggs and carefully placed them onto my plate, trying not to break the yolk. I loved dipping my toast in the runny stuff. I grabbed the toast and knife and slathered them with butter. I picked up four or five pieces of bacon and proceeded to the table. "Don't worry, Tank. I didn't forget you," I said, as I placed another slice of bacon onto the floor.

There's nothing better than a full belly. I was exhausted after my busy morning and the boys trespassing on my land. "Tank, come on boy. Let's get a nap."

TWENTY-ONE

Sunday, June 8, 1975

I woke to the sound of scratching at my door. Tank was trying to tell me he needed to go to the bathroom. I tossed the blankets off the bed, slid my feet into my slippers, and walked to the front door to let him out. He bolted for the front yard. I stood and watched him go from tree to plant to another tree. *What a simple life: eat, sleep, and pee anywhere you like.* I smiled.

I turned, looked over my shoulder, and peered down the hallway toward Bobby's room. I thought I heard a noise. I had an uneasy feeling brewing inside. I remembered what Gladys said yesterday: the spirits are back. The last time I went into Bobby's room, Donald Thornhill appeared. I heard a child's giggle as I approached. I placed my hand on the doorknob. It was cold. I knew what that meant. I twisted the knob and pushed the door open a few inches. So far, so good. Nothing seemed out of place. "Daddy," a faint voice said. I looked from side to side. I was the only person in the room.

I snapped out of it when I heard barking at the door. This made two days in a row that Tank had helped me. It's hard to believe how quickly I was falling for this little guy. I walked out and opened the door for Tank. He dashed down the hallway and growled at the entrance to Bobby's room. They said animals have a sixth sense, something humans didn't possess. I never entirely believed that, but they must be right because Tank knew something wasn't right in Bobby's room. I stood over Tank. "What do you see, boy?" He growled in response. "Do you see something or feel someone's in here?" *Look at me, talking to my dog like he understood everything I was saying.*

Tank slowly moved forward, and I was only a step behind. He sniffed and growled at the closet door. I took the lead and looked at what was behind door number one. *Okay, I watch too many game shows on TV.*

My palms were sweaty. My fingers trembled as I reached for the handle. Tank's growl grew louder. He was ready to pounce on whatever was about to come out. "Is that you, Daddy?" I jolted backward, almost stepping on Tank, who did a quick spin to get out of my way. Tank was locked on whatever was behind the door.

"Did you get me a puppy?" The soft tone was definitely Bobby's voice. Tank moved back, as did I.

How in the world did he know there was a dog in the house? Could ghosts see and hear everything around them? Did they have feelings? Did they care what we did or didn't do? All the signs were pointing in that direction. I forgot what it felt like to experience a spirit in the house. It was pretty unnerving. I wasn't sure how I was going to handle this again. The past ten-plus years had been relatively peaceful. I liked it that way. I missed April and Bobby, but the unknown really scared me.

Tank inched closer, moving in for the kill. *Ah, just open it*. I quickly snatched the handle, pulled the door open, and stepped back, letting Tank do all the work. A cold gush of air flowed over us and sent shivers down my spine. I couldn't move. Tank held his position. Bobby's translucent figure sat cross-legged on the closet floor. *He hadn't aged*. He was still ten years old, just like I remembered. He was holding a plastic dinosaur—the one I had bought him at the World's Fair. "Thank you, Dad, I love it," Bobby said, waving the dino back and forth. He even made a growl like the T-rex would, and Tank jumped around a little as if he was ready to play.

"What's his name?"

"Oh, I'm sorry. This is Tank," I said, rubbing his head.

"So now you get a dog?" Bobby said in an unpleasant tone. "Do you think you can replace me with a dog?" he yelled, and I could tell he was upset.

"No, no, I could never replace you. You're my son."

"Then why am I like this?" Bobby said, frustrated. He tried to pat Tank on the back. But his hand passed through him, and Tank spun and ran out of the room.

Bobby blinked in and out, fading before my eyes. "I'm sorry, Bobby. I never meant for any of this to happen. I wish I could go back in time and fix this mistake. I love you more than anything," I said, trying to get the words out before he evaporated. But it was too late. Bobby was gone. I hoped he could still hear what I said because I meant every word. I wished I could have a do-over.

Tank rubbed my pant leg as tears rolled down the side of my face. Tank whimpered a little. He was trying to comfort me. *I wished I would have gotten a dog a whole lot sooner. I didn't want to be alone anymore.*

I finished the bacon with an excellent bacon, lettuce, and tomato sandwich. Tank even convinced me to let him have a piece of bacon. It was safe to say he was getting spoiled. I was ready to lie down and get my afternoon nap when I heard a car door slam outside, and Tank bolted to the door and began to bark.

I pulled the curtain back and noticed Tom getting out of his car. This was an unexpected surprise. I guess the news of me shooting my gun off found its way to Tom rather quickly. Well, I'd tell him the truth. I pulled the knob and opened the door. "Hey Tom, what a nice surprise seeing you today," I said in a cheery tone. I didn't want him to think anything was wrong. I wanted to get this conversation off to a good start, not a sour one.

Tom entered and never said a word. His bloodshot eyes told me something was seriously wrong. *Oh, no… I sure hoped something hadn't happened to Gladys. I wasn't sure I could handle the bad news.*

Tom sat on the couch and gazed at me, doing his best not to make eye contact. "Tom, can I get you something to drink?"

"No thanks," Tom whispered and shook his head.

I took a seat next to Tom. "What's going on? I can tell something is wrong," I said. I was concerned. I had never seen Tom like this. What in the world could have upset him so much?

"Did something happen to Gladys?" I asked.

"No," Tom could barely get the word out.

I laid my hand on his shoulder. "Tom, what's going on? You're scaring me," I said.

"Sorry," he whimpered. My thoughts were all over the place. *It wasn't Gladys. Tom had no wife or a girlfriend, so those options were ruled out. Oh no…was Tom sick?*

"Talk to me, please. The suspense is killing me. What's going on?" I said, pleading my case for information.

"Jimmy." Tom managed to say.

That caught me off guard. "Jimmy, who works for you at the store?"

"He's gone." Tom said, and I watched a tear trace down his cheek.

"He quit?" I said and paused, and Tom started to cry. I patted him on the shoulder some more. "I'm sure you will find another kid to help out after school and in the summer." I smiled.

"No, he's dead," Tom said as he leaned forward and wrapped his arms around me.

I wasn't sure what to say. *I didn't see that coming. I just saw him yesterday, here at the house. He and his buddies were floating down the creek. How in the world could he be gone?* I patted Tom on the back. "I'm so sorry, Tom. I know he was a good kid, and he meant a lot to you and the store," I said, holding Tom a little longer. "How did it happen?"

Tom wiped his face on my shoulder and inhaled. "He drowned," Tom whispered. "He went over the axe factory dam," Tom said as he sobbed a little more, and I patted him on the back again.

Comforting people was not my strong suit. It's something I hated doing. Yet, Tom was there for me when April and Bobby passed away, so I needed to be here for Tom.

"Mr. Brooker called me this morning to let me know what happened to Jimmy. He knew Jimmy was supposed to work this afternoon. It took a lot of courage to call and explain what happened." Tom sobbed some more. "Sorry. Thanks for letting me get this off my chest," Tom said.

"No apology needed. Can I get you a Pepsi or glass of water?" I asked. Not waiting for his reply, I darted to the kitchen, grabbed a Pepsi, popped the top, and sat it on the coffee table. I proceeded to the bathroom to grab the facial tissue box and sat it next to Tom's soda. Tom nodded in gratitude. *I was stunned Jimmy Brooker died yesterday. Did these kids have something to do with waking the spirit world? There had to be some connection.* I watched Tom cry. Yes, I was sad, but not like Tom. He and Jimmy had worked together for almost a year, I guess.

The moments passed, and after the tears stopped, Tom was ready to shed some light on some details. It was an exciting story. Jimmy and his friends had spent the day floating down Fishing Creek. But I already knew that because I chased them off my property and downstream.

"They stopped at the bridge down the road from your house to jump off and swim," Tom mentioned. *I didn't know why these kids didn't start there when they decided to float downstream.* "They continued back to camp, only stopping at Jimmy's house for a few snacks and a break. That was the last time his parents saw him alive." Tom said.

I bet those boys were up to no good at the lumber yard. I heard stories about how Jimmy or one of those kids would steal or hide the worker's shoes or take someone's

*lunch. We never did anything like that when we were kids—
today's youth.*

"The boys pulled out of the water at their campsite. Only
Jimmy stayed on his raft and continued to float downstream.
That's where things get a little confusing," Tom leaned
toward me and whispered. "The Malone boy told the police
Jimmy was in some trance like he was possessed. I'm not a
hundred percent sure what he was talking about. But I kind
of have an idea. Do you remember the other morning when
you came to the store? I mentioned I felt weird. I think I
may have been in a trance myself. It felt like someone took
over my body and brain," Tom said.

"How is that even possible?" *I could not believe what I
was hearing. Even Tom has lost his mind.*

"We have both seen ghosts. Right?" Tom gave me a
side-eye. "So, explain that!" Tom said, making an excellent argument for his case, one I could not explain or dis-
agree with.

"Besides, it's not the first time I have felt like my body
has been taken over," Tom added.

"You're just telling me now? Does your mom know?" I
asked. *I couldn't believe Tom would hold information from
me. I'd been honest with him, well, almost.*

"Have you talked to your mom about this?" I asked.
"Maybe she can explain this better."

"Not yet. I'm still trying to process the fact that Jimmy
is gone," Tom said.

"Do you think there is a connection between these boys
and the spirit world?" I asked. Tom gave me a blank stare.

"Why Jimmy? Was it an accident? Or was he forced to
kill himself by a spirit like Donald Thornhill?" I said.

"Great work, Bob. Now I'm more confused. Maybe Mom can help us sort out this mess," Tom said.

I guess we were going to visit Gladys.

TWENTY-TWO

Saturday, June 14, 1975

We stopped to visit Gladys last weekend, and she had no answers for us, only more questions. She needed time to do her investigation. I didn't know if that included talking to the dead or not, but I was looking forward to seeing her today to see how everything was going.

I spent most of the week thinking about the connection between Jimmy and the spirit world. Someone had to know something. At the moment, no one was talking, at least not yet. But this was a small town, and secrets didn't stay hidden for long. Maybe I would get some answers today at the funeral home. Yes, that's an odd place to question whether or not people believed in ghosts. But I was a strange fellow, and the older I got, the less I cared what people thought about me.

I buttoned my shirt, tucked it into my dress slacks, and zipped up. Only a necktie stood between me and a funeral. April used to help me with the tie. Now, I struggled to put it on. I removed the tie and then tried again. I repeated this process several times and finally realized this was as good as it would get. *So what if it was a little crooked?* I gave Tank some extra food and made sure he went potty before I left the house. I was dragging my heels a little. Going to a funeral was something I didn't want to do. But I needed to be there for Tom and Gladys.

"Be careful, Bob," April whispered in my ear. I spun faster than a top, almost throwing out my back in the process. I stared at an empty room. I was positive it was April's voice, but it could have been Donald Thornhill. He had played me once before. I wouldn't put anything past that old fart. I knelt, rubbed Tank on the head, informing him to look out for nasty old Thornhill, and instructed Tank to bite, should he appear.

I drove slowly to the funeral home. I didn't see a single car on the road. *That was odd.* I rounded the corner and turned down the main street where the funeral home was located. I was stunned the streets were lined with cars. After driving in circles for ten minutes, I concluded that finding an empty parking place had turned into a night-mare. I noticed a young couple leaving and trailed them to their parked location. *I was sure they thought I was up to no good. I only wanted their parking spot.* Another car had the same idea, but they realized I was doing the same and backed off. I finally got the car parked. I locked the door and walked three blocks to the funeral home.

The massive crowds overflowed outside onto the sidewalks. I noticed Nurse Betty standing by herself. *Maybe things didn't work out with her and the doctor. She looked lovely in her black dress.* "Hi Bob," she said, waiving me over.

As I approached, she extended her arms to my neck. I wondered if she was going to hug me or even kiss me. My heart skipped a beat. She gently grabbed my necktie. "Let me help you with this," Betty said, grinning and showing me her perfect teeth. She straightened my tie for me, then retied it. "That looks much better, Bob. It's so nice to see you again," Betty added.

"You look so happy and stunning, like always," I said, giving her a cheesy grin. I watched her blush, and I felt like a schoolboy again.

"Thank you, Bob." She waved her left hand in front of my face, showing me the extra-large diamond ring on her finger. "Michael and I married a few months ago." She smiled.

"I don't see the doc in the crowd," I mentioned. I was reeling from the blow to my heart. *I needed to move on. I bet the ring cost more than my car was worth. She was out of my league and now a married woman. You never cross that line.*

"He should be here shortly; he's parking the car."

"Well, nice to see you again. Thanks for straightening my tie. If you will excuse me, I need to find my friends," I said. I nudged my way through the crowd while mentioning I was family. Hey, a little lie never hurt anyone. I managed to get past the doorway. I scratched my name in the visitor logbook for the family. *Dang, I could not believe I was on page seven. Everyone in town must be here.*

I noticed some of the guys who worked at the Salona Stone Quarry gathered in the corner; they were chatting away. I couldn't tell you how many of their cars and trucks I had worked on over the years. A few nodded in my direction, and I did the same. I elbowed my way through the lumberjack boys. Most of these guys worked at the lumber mill in Salona on Lizardville Road. As I squeezed past, I heard one of them saying how Jimmy used to cause so much trouble around the mill—stealing lunches and messing with people's work gear—just a real pain in the behind. One even said he would not miss him. Someone else mentioned karma.

I didn't care how many childish pranks you pulled; no one deserved to die. And think about his parents. They were the ones who would suffer the most—wondering how they had failed as parents. I knew all about grief. I lost my wife and son. I was in the hospital when they buried April and Bobby. I wasn't sure why, but I'd never stopped by the cemetery to visit them. Maybe it was because they were buried in her family plot next to her grandparents. I wanted to say hello, but I could not find the strength to visit. Maybe it was because I didn't want to chance running into any of her family members. Maybe the real reason I never went to see them was the fact that they were still living in my house, well, sort of.

There were kids galore, nestled next to their parents, trying to understand what had happened and why. I think every kid from school was here, including many of their teachers. This was what happened when a child died. You had large crowds. *I bet Tom would be the only one to come and pay his respects when I pass.* I continued to push my way forward nicely. I spotted our local rent-a-cop, as I called him. Then I turned my back to him so he would not notice me as I shuffled along. I was only assuming the other boys never filed a complaint about my firing my rifle that day. Jimmy's death changed things for everyone. I looked down the aisle. There was a small wooden coffin with a large picture centered on top. Flowers lined the hall on both sides. There wasn't an empty seat in the house.

I noticed an arm waving at me. It was Tom. He and Gladys had saved me a seat in the third row. Great, I wanted to hide back here and kind of blend in, if that was possible. Now, I would sit three rows behind Jimmy's parents. I inched my way forward until I reached my seat. I extended my arm and hugged Gladys, then shook Tom's hand and thanked him for saving me a spot.

"Have you learned anything yet?" I asked Gladys.

"Bob, this is not the place nor the time," Gladys said, her voice firm.

"Maybe after the services, we can all grab lunch and chat," Tom whispered.

The front row of seats fell silent, followed by the second row, then our row. Each row went silent as the pastor passed by, approaching the altar. The wave of silence continued out of the hall and into the streets.

We rose, prayed, and did what we were told. The service was nice and elegant, lasting about twenty minutes. There was plenty of tissue used to wipe up the tears. Everyone took their cue when Mr. and Mrs. Brooker rose, hugged, and shook hands with everyone attending Jimmy's funeral. They were working their way to Gladys, Tom, and me. My hand was already feeling numb and clammy. If I had to do another handshake, I was going to scream. I grasped Mr. Brooker's hand. He had a firm shake for a man who just lost his only son. I said my condolences and Mrs. Brooker wrapped her arms around me and hugged me. "I'm sorry for your loss," I whispered before she released me and moved to Tom, then Gladys.

It was nice getting out of the house for a change. *Seeing Nurse Betty and hugging Mrs. Brooker was the most action I'd had in some time— alright, fourteen years to be exact. Why did I have these strange thoughts? I guess I was lonely.*

We worked our way to the front of the building. I noticed those hooligans huddled in the corner—the Malone brothers, Parker's siblings, and a few other strays I didn't recognize. I made eye contact with Johnny, the youngest Malone boy. He shot me the stink eye. I was sure he thought I was the devil himself. I wrinkled my nose and gritted my teeth in return.

"What are you doing?" Tom asked sarcastically.

"Nothing," I snarled.

"I saw you make a face at Johnny." Tom shook his head.

"Did not," I lied.

"Grow up, you two," Gladys whispered harshly.

The crowds thinned quickly. We stood on the sidewalk for a moment, deciding where to have lunch. Gladys suggests the Dutch Inn. I reminded her we would need reservations, but Gladys said not to worry. We moseyed down the street, talking about the large turnout and how sad it was that a young man had lost his life. It made me think of my Bobby. *Taken before he even had a chance to live life and experience how wonderful this world could be.* I missed him, but I didn't share with anyone that I saw him this morning.

I held the door for Gladys and Tom. I was surprised at how busy they were. I guess everyone had the same idea. The waiting room was packed. I was ready to grumble about how long we would have to wait when the hostess motioned us to follow. I guess Gladys had some pull in certain circles. They ushered us to a small, private room in the back. The waiter quickly brought us our drinks. I was ready to change the conversation to finding out who had woken up the spirit world, when an old gentleman using a cane entered the room.

"Leonardo," Gladys said as she stood and hugged him. The two conversed in another language. I thought it was Italian, but I could have been wrong.

Leonardo pulled out Gladys's chair, helped her to her seat, then pulled out his chair. The waiter returned quickly and placed a salad before each of us, including Leonardo.

"This is Leonardo. He's the owner and a close friend," Gladys said, giving a smug smile.

"It's nice to meet you," I said, and Tom followed suit. *I was going to turn sixty in a few years, and I was just finding this out now. I could have eaten here more often had I known I didn't need to make reservations.*

"Boys, just call me Leo." He paused. "Let me guess…" He placed his finger on the side of his forehead and closed his eyes for a few seconds. "You want to talk about the awakening?" His voice was raspy, and his speech slow.

"Well, I think Bob has a few questions, as do I," Gladys answered.

"How did you know about the awakening," I asked curiously.

"I feel everything. I know all. Need I say more?" Leo said.

"Um, okay," I said, puzzled.

"Let me tell you what I know." He nodded. "Yes, I felt it too. Just like the day you and Mabel cast the spell." He smiled and waved his finger at Gladys. "I felt it before they were awakened. The minute the Parker boy started telling the story, I knew they would wake. See, it happened a long time ago—a mass murder with missing bodies. It's the legend of the ax factory murders, and no one should ever talk about it." Leo said. "But that's not all. Someone has something that they should not—something that belongs to another. The two things together add up to the awakening."

This old man was talking in circles. I wasn't sure what he was talking about, but I noticed Tom fidgeting in his chair. I wasn't the only one who noticed. "I think we know who the guilty party is," Leo said.

So, Tom knew what he was talking about? I hated being the last to know things. "Tom, what am I missing?" I asked with a hint of urgency.

Leo and Gladys stared at Tom until he cracked. "I don't know anything about the story that was told. I swear." He placed his hand over his heart. "I only let Jimmy hold the puzzle box," Tom said, awaiting our response. "We were trying to see if we could get it open." Tom made eye contact with each of us. "Did I get Jimmy killed? I never meant to hurt anyone, let alone get Jimmy killed." Tom took a few deep breaths, waiting for some sort of response.

I noticed Gladys was eating her salad, so I grabbed my fork and did the same. "How can you eat after all I have done?" Tom spilled his guts before us. "This is all my fault." Tom cupped his hands over his face.

"Everything will be fine," Leo said, breaking the silence. "We need you to get the puzzle box back for safekeeping." Leo took a bite out of his salad.

"Do you think the puzzle box killed Jimmy?" I took another bite of the delicious salad. *This dressing must be from a homemade recipe.* Tom stared at me as if I had accused him of killing Jimmy. "It's not your fault. How were you to know?" I added, so Tom would relax.

"I don't think the box had anything to do with his death, but it may have played a small role," Leo said, returning to his food. Tom may have lost his appetite because he sat, only picking at his food, which was unlike Tom.

The waiter placed a double-decker club sandwich in front of me. *Oh, that looked scrumptious. I couldn't wait to dive in.* I knew I was in heaven the second I took my first bite. The bread was so soft, with just the right amounts of meat, lettuce, and tomatoes; and there was that salad dressing again.

We ate and enjoyed our meal, and the waiter returned, gathered the plates, and refilled our drinks. I felt like a turkey at Thanksgiving—stuffed! Finally, Tom cleared his throat, breaking the silence. "I never meant to hurt Jimmy. I'm so sorry," he said, shaking his head. "I'm not sure I can get the puzzle box back. It would be at Jimmy's house," he said.

"If you like, I can go with you for support," I added, dabbing the napkin around my mouth.

"It doesn't matter how you do it. It would be best if you got the box back in your family," Leo said. "One more thing… when you retrieve the box, keep it safe." Leo pushed away from the table. Gladys rose to her feet, gave him one final hug, and thanked him for lunch.

"It was nice meeting you boys," Leo said. He turned with the cane in hand and staggered out of the room.

The waiter returned and started to clear the table. I requested my bill, and he laughed. "Sir, you're all set. Thank you for dining with us today." He smiled and returned to the kitchen. I thanked him and told him to thank Leo, too.

While I walked to the car, the only thing I could think about was why in the world Tom would let Jimmy have the puzzle box. I hadn't seen that stupid box in ten years and didn't want to see it again. But, if it helped us close the spirit world, then I was all for it.

TWENTY-THREE

Wednesday, August 27, 1975

It had been a little over two months since Jimmy's passing. I was annoyed by some of the things that had happened. First, Tom was not able to get the puzzle box back. So, the spirit world was still open and active. Now I heard Bobby playing again and April cooking in the kitchen, and here's a new one. One morning, I woke up to the sound of the shower running. I heard April getting ready, and she told me to hurry, or we would be late. When I opened the bathroom door, the room was empty. But the shower was running. Tank lay on the floor watching. *Sometimes, I wanted to be a dog. All I would have to do then was eat, sleep, and play.*

Something else that bothered me was that Tom hired Johnny Malone to work part-time at the store. I wasn't sure what he was thinking. Tom had also been acting strangely lately. Not to mention, he'd only been to my house twice in the past ten weeks. I told him about the Malone kid, but he wouldn't listen. Other strange things had been going on, too. The lights flickered off and on several times a week. That was something new. Tank barked at odd hours of the night. He sensed paranormal activity when it occurred in the house. That alerted me to when they were present.

Tank had also grown and put on several pounds. He's happy, healthy, and extremely playful. He's my new best friend. If I didn't know better, I would have thought Tom was trying to put some distance between the two of us. Maybe that's why he got me a dog.

Monday through Friday, it's off to work and then home. Same old dull routine every day. I was becoming a hermit, and I liked it that way. The sun was setting, and tonight would be a great evening. It was a quiet night alone with Tank until I heard a car door slam. I snapped to attention. I wasn't expecting anyone.

I darted to the front window, pulled the curtain back, and noticed Tom walking up the stairs. I opened the door, and Tom blew right past me and started pacing back and forth.

"Oh gosh, now what have you done?" I said quizzically.

"Nothing, I swear. Well, sort of, but it was not my fault," Tom answered.

"Please don't tell me you made matters worse," I said, a hint of panic in my voice.

"Listen for a minute," Tom said, pacing. Then he walked over to the refrigerator, opened the door, and grabbed two bottles of Pepsi.

"Sure, just help yourself," I said sarcastically.

Tom opened the bottles; his hands shook as he placed one in front of me and took a large gulp from his bottle before setting it down onto the coffee table. I noticed the dirt on the knees of his trousers. *What has he gotten himself into this time? I knew by the way he was acting something was wrong. The last time he acted this way, someone had died.*

"Please don't tell me someone died?" I blurted out before thinking.

"What the heck?" Tom said, yelling back. "Nobody died, and I don't like your tone."

"You're right. I'm sorry," I said, leaning back on the couch, ready to listen to what Tom said. "The floor is all yours." I waved my hands in front of me.

"Alright, where to begin?" Tom squirmed in his seat. "Let's go back to the funeral when we had lunch with my mom and Leo. Since then, I've been practicing and reading how to cast spells and sorts."

"So, you want to be a witch?" I asked. I could not believe my ears.

"Hardly. I would be a wizard," Tom replied and smiled. "Strange things have been happening. I mean, I have been able to cast a few small spells. I moved a penny with my mind and almost lit a candle by myself. Mom said it's going to take many years of practice. But what else do I have to do with my time? Oh, there have been a few times where I blacked out. I think I was possessed. I know it can happen. Spirits can channel into your body and use you." Tom grew excited.

"I'm happy for you if that is what you want," I added with a long glare.

"Let me continue. After lunch that day, Leo told me it was important to get the puzzle box back and keep it close. I failed!" Tom shook his head and continued. "I went to visit Mr. and Mrs. Brooker. I explained what I was looking for and that it was an old family keepsake. They knew exactly what I was talking about. They said Jimmy had placed a note on the box with Johnny's name on it, so they left the box to Johnny because they thought it was his," Tom said.

"Are you telling me that Johnny Malone has the puzzle box?" *I wasn't sure why he didn't take the box back, but he didn't. He's a better man than I.*

"Yes, that is why I hired him; I've been trying to keep the box close to me. I figured if I gave Johnny a job, I could keep a close watch on the box. And if they could figure out what it contained, I would be the first person he would tell. And I was right, well kind of," Tom added. "He also told me that the day before Jimmy drowned, Parker told the others that night about the legend of the Ax Factory Murders. After that, weird things began to happen to the boys. I know for sure they woke up the spirit world," Tom said.

"One more thing: Johnny was able to open the box. It emitted a cloud that took shape and offered a clue."

My mouth hung open; *the kid was able to figure out how to open the puzzle box. Of course, he would outsmart all the adults. He's a lucky little brat.* "So, what was the clue?"

"At first, he didn't share the clue with me, so I followed him and kept close tabs on his movements, along with his brother Buck. It was smart of me to do so because it ultimately paid off. The clues pointed them to a remote spot in the woods. If you take the Hallows in the valley and follow the trail to the top, you will find a small pond and waterfall. Where the water cascades down the rocks, there is a cave. It's hidden quite well. You can't find the entrance without moving some of the brush. It's a small crack in the wall. But once you enter, the cave opens to a large tunnel.

"Johnny wanted the day off this past Saturday, and I knew he was up to something. I followed him that morning, and when I spotted all the kids gathering at the Parker house, I knew something was going down. The group left, heading up the mountain. I trailed them to the top, where the waterfall was. They had no clue I was there. I found two of them sitting outside while the others went inside the cave to explore," Tom said.

"I hate to interrupt, but isn't that the pond and cave we found when we were kids?" I asked.

"Yes, it was," Tom said. He was acting like he had never been there before.

"Okay, I was just curious," I said, asking Tom to continue. He nodded.

"A commotion broke out, and I heard screaming and yelling coming from inside the cave. Sara Parker and one of the boys hustled to the entrance, and I watched them all appear, except for Johnny. Finally, he showed up, and they were all mad at him for playing some sort of prank. I'm glad he did because that's when the entire group went inside the cave, allowing me the opportunity to follow them inside. Don't worry, I kept my distance. Their voices echoed off the walls, and I could hear everything they talked about," Tom said, taking another gulp of his soda pop.

I listened to everything Tom talked about. I was unsure if I should believe all this garbage, but I didn't believe in ghosts fourteen years ago. "What was in the cave?"

"Ah, man, that's where this gets wild. I followed the group down to some small area. Another extension of the cave was on the left-hand side of the wall. They ducked inside. They found an old shovel and began to dig, and after some time, they found skeletal remains. You know they never found Annabelle or Jacob after they went missing back in the day."

"I see someone has been brushing up on his local history," I said and nodded.

"Yep, anyway, a couple of ghosts appeared. Not just any ghosts— Annabelle and Jacob, to be exact. They warned the kids not to disturb the grave, or there would be consequences. So the boys quickly covered the grave, and we all left."

"Is that it?" I asked.

"Yep," Tom replied.

"You didn't leave anything out. Like, where is the puzzle box now?"

"Well, I kind of buried the box in the grave."

"You what? Man, what are you thinking? Leo told you to keep it close to you if we wanted to close the spirit world again. Come on, Tom, why?" I questioned his judgment.

"It's not like that," Tom insisted.

"Please tell me what it's like," I said with a snarl.

"I'm trying to please you, my mother, and the kids. Can you give me a break?" Tom said, almost begging.

"Fine, I sure hope you know what you are doing because, personally, I think you are playing with fire and about to get burned," I said.

"Bob, please, I need you to trust me," Tom said. His expression showed me how much he believed his actions were right.

"Okay, cuz, I trust you. Please don't disappoint me," I added.

Tom changed the subject and finished his soda before heading for the door. I let Tank go out for a bit so he could do his business, then called it a night.

TWENTY-FOUR

I deserved a good night's sleep. I woke fresh, and my mind was clear. That's better than the past few nights where I tossed and turned. Don't get me wrong; it still troubled me, the thought of Johnny Malone with the puzzle box. To top it off, he was able to open it and figure out the clue. I wanted to stop by the store and confront him when he was working. I was sure Tom would not approve of it, so I kept my distance.

Something wasn't sitting right with me. *How did they do it? A group of young kids solving a seventy-year-old missing person case? Why didn't they call the police?* Never mind. With this town having a rent-a-cop, I didn't blame them. I wouldn't call the police, either. I guess I'd have to trust Tom.

The first thing for me was to let Tank outside so he could do his business. I stood on the porch and watched; he wasn't long, which made me smile. I hauled my butt into the bathroom with Tank on my heels. "No, boy, you're not getting in here today," I said as I pushed him away. I turned on the water and climbed into the shower. The hot water felt great, running over my body. Tank barked at the door. "I'm not letting you in," I hollered back. After a few minutes, I rinsed and turned the water off. I reached outside the shower and grabbed my towel. I dried off, stepped out, and froze in my tracks. Goosebumps broke out all over my body. I wobbled and placed my hand on the sink to steady myself. I stared at the mirror dripping in condensation. "Help me" was etched on the glass mirror. It looked like someone had taken their finger to the mirror. Was this why Tank was barking?

I opened the bathroom door, and Tank burst in and barked at the mirror. He did know. I was not surprised. "Good boy." I patted him on the head.

I knew I had locked the front door. There was no way someone could have entered the house and done this. I wrapped my towel around me and walked up front to double-check. I froze in my tracks. I gawked at the chairs turned upside down on the kitchen table. I glanced at the door. "Yes," I said. It was locked.

I remembered April would place the chairs like this when she mopped the floor. This had to be April's doing. *But who would be asking for my help? Could this be April? Or Bobby? Or another prank by Donald Thornhill?* I was getting frustrated. Things had been so peaceful for so long. I started to feel like I was losing my mind again. But I knew inside I wasn't. It was the spirit world messing with me. Since those dang kids awakened the spirit world, this stuff kept happening. I needed to get to the bottom of this and send the spirits back. I needed to take this matter into my own hands. I had to finish what was started.

I walked back to the bathroom and wiped my mirror with my towel. I went to my bedroom, dressed, and decided I needed to check out this cave to get the remains and move them to the cemetery. I hoped this would stop the madness. Tank stayed underfoot as I paced back and forth. I grabbed and placed each chair back where they belonged.

I needed a backpack, a shovel, and a flashlight or two. I also needed a big duffle bag to put the remains inside. If I was going to do this, I needed to do it today and get it over with. I had most of what I needed, but I would need to run into town to buy a large duffle bag.

I finished things around the house, said goodbye to Tank, and climbed into the car. The car roared to life, and I drove down Lizardville Road. I continued over the first bridge and then moved slowly past Tom's General Store. I spotted Tom's Mustang and Johnny's bike leaning against the wall. I continued to make my way toward the hardware store in town. I was sure they would have precisely what I was looking for.

Things were quiet for a Saturday morning. I parked out front and made my way inside the store. "Good morning, Bob. How can we help you today?" Larry said with a smile.

Larry and I went to school together when we were kids. He was the captain of the football team, the jock that all the girls wanted to date. I was sure April tried to date him, too. *Look at him now, working at the hardware store, sporting a nice beer belly.* I remembered seeing him all the time at the Linger Inn Tavern. They had a saying around the bar: "linger in and stumble out." *Those were the good ol' days. I lost my beer belly. I guess that was what happened when you stopped drinking.* "Hello Larry, good seeing you again," I said, knowing that was a lie.

"You too, Bob." He looked confused. "Can I help you find something?"

"Yes, I'm looking for a heavy-duty duffle bag, something large enough to put a body in," I said and laughed.

"We don't have a lot of folks asking for large, heavy-duty body bags these days," Larry replied with a chuckle. "I do have this baby. I followed Larry down two aisles and around the corner. He stopped and held up a large green canvas sack with a zipper. It had to be almost four feet in length. And deep enough to put plenty of tools inside. *Yes, it should be large enough to hold human remains.*

Larry handed me the bag, and I studied it, and the size and bag seemed sturdy enough for what I needed to do. "I think this will work. I should be able to put plenty of tools inside," I added to make sure I didn't draw suspicion to myself.

I handed the bag back to Larry and walked behind as we made our way to the cash register. I pulled my wallet out and gave Larry a twenty. Larry rang me up and handed me my change, and I was on my way home in a flash.

I slowed as I drove past the Parker residence. I noticed the girls hanging out back, and some of the boys were there, too. Several cars were in the driveway, telling me they had company. I couldn't sneak past the house today with everyone around. I would need to wait for the right time.

Days passed, and it turned into weeks. I was growing frustrated. Whenever I tried to find the cave, something happened at the house. Then the weather changed. Winter came early this year, and I was not about to go hiking in the mountains when it was cold and snowy. The tracks alone would be a dead giveaway. It looked like I would have to wait for spring to make my move.

TWENTY-FIVE

Saturday, May 15, 1976

We had one of the worst winters on record, with so much snow that I was tired of plowing my driveway. The riding mower with the plow I purchased came in handy. I was excited spring had finally arrived. I used my time wisely over the winter. I stopped by the Lizardville Cemetery several times in the past few weeks and found exactly what I was looking for—Donald Thornhill's grave. Spots were reserved for his wife, Annabelle, and their daughter. I made a small plaque on the ground next to their site and knew I needed to dig a grave for the remains I would retrieve from the mountain. While I was speaking with Tom yesterday, he mentioned the Parker family was out of town for the weekend. This was my chance.

It was a cool, crisp morning, and a light fog covered the yard. I woke early and made my way to the cemetery. I drove along the side fence and parked around the back near the tree line. No one could see me from the road, and even if they spotted my car, they would think I was visiting April and Bobby. The chances of anyone stopping here were slim.

I sat quietly for a few moments, my heart racing. *I was getting too old for this stuff.* I got up the nerve, opened the door, popped the trunk, and grabbed my pick and shovel. I laid them on the ground next to Donald Thornhill's grave. I placed my right hand in my pocket to make sure I had the stone Gladys gave me for protection. I smiled when I felt the smooth surface on my fingers.

I picked up the shovel and removed the top layer of grass. When I was finished, I needed to place these back on top so it would not look like a new grave site. I was pleasantly surprised there were only a few rocks, and I didn't need the pick to break up the soil. The digging went quickly. I was four or five feet down and decided that was enough. I would leave this alone until I returned with the remains. I felt confident no one would find this since they hadn't buried anyone here in years.

I returned the pick and shovel to the car trunk and closed the lid. I couldn't leave without saying hi to April and Bobby. Fifteen years, and this would be the first time I stopped to say hello. I strolled toward the front of the cemetery and found them where I expected them to be— in her family's plot. I stopped and stood over their graves. Two empty spaces were reserved for April's mother and father, and next to them were their beloved daughter, April Smithers, and grandson, Bobby Smithers, next to her—no room for me. A warm tear traced down my cheek. "I'm sorry for everything. For all the pain and suffering I caused you. I'm going to fix everything. Well, I'm going to try." I stepped away, paused, and turned to face their tombstones. "I love you, April and Bobby. I miss you both so much.

I wish I could hold you both in my arms and tell you in person," I said, trying to suppress my emotions. I had to stay focused and complete my mission. I turned and walked as quickly to the car as I could. I was riddled with guilt.

I went straight home and cleaned up, then let Tank outside for a bit, drove to the ax factory dam, and parked in a secluded spot. If anyone noticed the car, they would think I was along the creek fishing, even though I did most of my fishing from my backyard. Most people would not know that. I popped the trunk, grabbed my backpack, and strapped it to my back. I brought a fold-up shovel to fit inside the pack along with the duffle bag. I checked both ways. No cars were in sight, and I sprinted across the road along the path that led to the mountain. I felt more at ease once I was past the Parker house and a few hundred yards into the woods.

I wasn't sure how long all of this was going to take. I paused a few times to drink water from my canteen. I was not in the shape I used to be in. Just as Tom had described doing, I trekked upward to the top of the mountain. I stopped several times, listening for the waterfalls—still nothing, so I continued forward. As I approached the two-hour mark, I finally heard running water, which made me smile. It was coming from my right. I left the path and pushed my way through the underbrush. After thirty yards or so, I stepped out into a clearing. *Wow, this was just as Tom had described it and just as I remembered it being as a child.* Water cascaded down some fifteen or twenty feet into a small pool of water. The pond couldn't have been ten or fifteen feet across, a great place for the animals to stop and refresh. I turned my attention behind me when I heard branches cracking. I focused, listening to birds chirping in the distance. This place was starting to give me the creeps. I noticed a few crows circling overhead. "Don't panic," I whispered to myself. I exhaled, moved to the wall, and searched for the hidden entrance. I was sure it wouldn't take long since Tom had told me where to find it. And I was correct.

I noticed some branches that were sort of out of place. I pulled them to the side and saw a large crack in the wall. *Bingo! I found it.* I pushed the debris out of my way, removed my backpack, and tossed it into the entrance. I heard squawking noises from behind as I placed one foot inside, then the other. I poked my head out, glanced around, and grabbed the brush and branches, pulling them over the entrance to conceal my whereabouts. That wasn't smart, as the cave plunged into darkness. But this would also keep anyone or any animal out while I was inside.

I took a few steps in and felt around for my backpack. I quickly unzipped the top pocket and pulled out a flashlight. It was much better being able to see where I was going. The cave surprised me. It opened into a large room. I shined my light around and began my descent. The floor was slippery in places, so I moved slowly. At one point, I wasn't sure if I had gone too far. The cave dropped steeply, but I remembered Tom saying something about that. I kept my eyes open, focusing on the left side. I stopped and smiled as I found the cavern on the left side of the tunnel, just as Tom had mentioned. I removed my backpack and squeezed through the tight space. I noticed loose dirt and knew this had to be the spot. I yanked a folding shovel from my pack and began to dig. It didn't take long before I hit something odd. I used my hands to clear more of the dirt. It was a blanket or tarp. I noticed a piece of wood and moved the ground to uncover the puzzle box—an awe-inspiring piece of woodwork, I might add. Next, I found the body. I wrapped the remains in an old blanket I had and stuffed it as best I could into the large duffle bag. *It was a good thing I had brought those with me. So far, everything was going according to plan. But when did my plans work out how they were supposed to? They usually didn't.*

I glanced around and decided to leave things the way they were. I wrapped the puzzle box and placed it into my backpack for safekeeping. I needed to get these remains to the cemetery and get him buried before someone or something realized what I was up to.

I started my climb back to the entrance. Everything was dead silent. I shivered and moved forward. I reached the bottom of the steep incline, tossed my backpack to the top, swung the duffle bag next, and let it fly up the ramp. I heard a crunching sound when it landed. It's good that whoever's remains they were could not feel pain. I backed up and took a running start. I slipped and slid but managed to claw my way up the steep incline.

I decided to catch my breath. I leaned against the wall and pulled my canteen from the bag. I gulped down three or four slugs of water. I was ready for a nap, but this was not the place or the time. One thing I forgot to bring was a watch. April hated that about me, and I smiled. *I never wore my watch on the weekends. Why would I? Who wants to keep track of time on their days off?* I had no idea how long I had been gone. It had to be mid-afternoon by now. I was hoping it wasn't later than that. I didn't want to be in the woods late at night. One thing I forgot to bring was insect repellant. The mosquitoes could eat you alive at dusk.

I rose to my feet and slipped the backpack over my shoulder. I grabbed the duffle bag strap and dragged the duffle bag behind me. I pushed forward a flashlight in one hand and the body bag in the other. I was wearing out again when I spotted a sliver of light coming from the entrance. I didn't remember that much light coming in before. I forced myself forward, one step at a time. I glanced around and found nothing and no one in sight. I stopped short of going outside. I pushed the brush to one side and stuffed the duffle bag through the opening, followed by the backpack. I spoke a few words Gladys had told me to say, grabbed the stone in my pants pocket, and moved them to my shirt pocket, keeping them close to my heart for protection. *Was I being silly for thinking a stone or pendant could protect me from a pissed-off ghost?* I guess the moment of truth had arrived. Carrying my pack, I plunged out into the sunlight. I gazed around the perimeter. The coast was clear. I grabbed the bag and headed for the path that would take me to my car. I noticed a few large crows fighting in the trees above and picked up my pace. The sun was to the west, which told me it was later than I thought. I needed to get a move on. One thing was certain: going downhill was easier than the climb I experienced earlier today.

I was starting to panic a little. I glanced around every tree and turned. I had this weird feeling rush over me that I was being followed. *Surely, I wasn't, but I was going to play it safe.* I continued my descent and walked at a vigorous pace. I was definitely out of shape. Just because I did a lot of yard work around the house didn't equate to being in top-notch condition. I was far from the perfect male specimen. I hurried along, wishing this day would soon end. But I still needed to get to the car, place the body in the ground, and cover it before I could go home.

I heard strange noises coming from behind me. I stopped and dropped the bag. I turned just in time to see two crows heading straight for me. I tripped over the bag, landing on my back with a thud. Pain seared down the back of my head, and I quickly moved my hand to the spot to check for blood—*nothing major from what I could tell*. An enormous crow flew in and began fighting with the smaller two. *Was I in the middle of a bird fight?* I scrambled to my feet, grabbed the sack, and started to trot down the mountain. I didn't know how long I could keep up this pace without a heart attack. *Boy, oh boy, wouldn't that look good in the newspaper: "Bob Smithers dies from a heart attack while carrying human remains in a duffle bag in the Basket Maker Hallows."* I chuckled on the inside. Yes, that was the nickname for this part of the woods—Basket Maker Hallows. They say a witch once lived in an old cottage somewhere in these woods. She used to weave and sell baskets at the local market on Saturdays. But that was way before my time. Tom and I heard the legends and never found anything that resembled a cottage.

I hurried as quickly as possible until I spotted a little water stream and knew I was approaching the Parker house. I paused momentarily to catch my breath, then continued cautiously past the house and stopped near Lizardville Road to ensure no cars were passing. The coast was clear, and I darted over the road and down the embankment toward my vehicle. I heard a car drive by just as I reached the rear of my Plymouth. I fumbled for my keys and slid them into the slot, turned the key, and opened the trunk. I tossed the backpack in first, followed by the duffle bag.

As I closed the trunk lid, I heard tires on the gravel road approaching my rear.

The car rolled to a stop. I was afraid to turn around because it might be our only local rent-a-cop. *How was I going to explain any of this to him?* "Hey Bob, funny running into you down here." I recognized the voice anywhere.

"Hi, Tom," I said as I turned around. His smile warmed my soul. *Be calm and act normal.*

"What brings you down here to the dam?" Tom questioned.

Quickly, I thought up a lie. "I thought the fish might be biting down here. I didn't have much luck at the house this morning." I nodded. "Just not a good day for fishing, I guess."

Tom scanned me up and down. "What happened?" He pointed to my clothes.

"Oh, this?" I pointed at myself. "I slipped on the bank. It was slick as snot. I almost fell into the water," I added to ensure Tom would believe me.

"Well, it's a good thing that didn't happen," Tom said, and I nodded. "So, what are you doing in a little bit? I can stop by, and we can catch up if you like," Tom asked.

"It's been a long day, Tom. I need to get home, feed Tank, and get a shower. I'll probably hit the sack early, if you know what I mean." Tom was buying my lies, which was good for me. I looked over Tom's shoulder and noticed several large crows perched on the power lines.

"If you like, swing by tomorrow anytime," I said, slowly moving toward the car door.

"Sure, sounds great. I'll see you tomorrow," Tom said, putting his car in reverse. I watched as he pulled away. I climbed into the front seat as the crows flew past my head. *What was up with these birds today? They were starting to get on my nerves. If I had my shotgun, I would pump them full of buckshot.*

I placed the car in drive and carefully pulled away. *I was not too fond of the fact that Tom spotted me down here. It tied me to the scene of the crime. But what crime? Who else knew of the remains of a human body? Tom. The kids. Yet no one had told the police. I decided I'd be fine.* I reasoned with myself as I drove straightaway to the cemetery.

I arrived quickly, glanced in all directions, then slowly pulled alongside the cemetery and drove to the rear. Once out of sight from the main road, I popped the trunk, grabbed the duffle bag and shovel, and darted to the hole. The sun was setting, and I had just enough light to finish this and be home before dark.

I tossed the bag into the hole and glanced down to ensure it was deep enough, and it was. I quickly started covering the bag. I didn't know I could move this quickly, and I was surprised I still had the strength to complete the task at hand. *Maybe I was in better shape than I thought.* I tossed the last few shovels of dirt on top. I quickly began to dance on top to pat the soil down. I grabbed the large pieces of sod and placed them on top and continued stomping on them. Things were looking great, and everything had gone just like I planned. I noticed four large crows flying in the distance, and they appeared to be fighting. Then there were three as one vanished before my eyes. Maybe my eyes played tricks on me, but I was sure I had counted four.

TWENTY-SIX

Saturday, July 24, 1976

The sun rose in the east. It was going to be a fabulous day. I decided to mow my yard before it got too hot outside. Tank chased me around on the mower. It was a game he and I played every weekend. I showered and changed clothes. Tank and I had lunch under the tree beside the water. *I loved living in the country.* I kicked back and let my mind wander.

It had been a little over two months since I pulled off the great body heist. I was so proud of myself. Even a man of my age could still accomplish a stealth mission. I guess watching war movies has paid off. The downside was that nothing had changed. I thought that taking those remains and burying them would put an end to all of this ghost stuff, but it didn't. Bobby and April were still with me. I hadn't seen them in a few weeks, but the board game and baseball glove still showed up like clockwork. I loved waking up to the smell of breakfast, even though when I went into the kitchen, there was no food. Now, that would be terrific if I could only teach April to make me breakfast. Not to push my luck, but if she could clean the dishes, too, my day would be complete.

I must have dozed off. I heard Tank barking, which startled me. When I looked up, he was chasing a few squirrels. "Good luck, Tank," I hollered. This was the life, the life April and I had dreamed of—spending our days relaxing and enjoying life, sharing our time with each other. Bobby would have turned twenty-five this year. He might have been married, and April and I could have been grandparents. That was our dream. "I miss you, April," I whispered to the wind. My eyes welled up. "Come on, Tank, time to go inside."

Tank followed me inside the house. I turned on the television and lay on the couch for my afternoon nap. Tank snuggled into me. I was startled when the phone rang. "Hello."

"Oh, hey Tom. Yes, I'll be home this evening." *I wasn't sure where else I would have been*. Monday through Friday consisted of work and a few trips to the store, but for the most part, I spent my weekends at the house. "That would be great. I'll see you in a little while."

I hadn't heard from Tom in a few weeks. He checked in occasionally, and I would stop by the store when I knew Johnny wasn't working. Tom told me Gladys hadn't been feeling well lately. I hoped nothing had happened to her, but she was getting up there in the years, so it was something I was expecting, and I thought Tom shared the same feelings. I had grown to like her. I decided to clean up a bit before Tom arrived. Maybe we could sit outside on the back porch and have iced tea instead of Pepsi.

Time slipped away, and before I knew it, I heard a car door close outside, followed by a second car door. Tom didn't mention bringing anyone else. I pulled back the curtain and frowned.

I opened the front door. "Hello Tom, nice to see you." I half smiled as he entered. Johnny Malone followed behind, and I motioned for him to come inside.

"Why'd you bring that bucket of nuts with you?" I chuckled as Johnny wrinkled his nose at me. I wasn't pleased that Tom brought him to my house without warning me first, but I was sure he had a reason for bringing him along.

"Well, we need to talk to you about something," Tom explained.

"What's he done now? Did you steal something from me? Didja boy?" He stared at me.

"No sir, I would never…" He paused. "We need your help," Johnny whispered as he gazed at the floor.

I tilted my head to the side, puzzled. *How could I help him?* "Where are my manners? Can I offer you something to drink?"

"Oh, you're asking me?" Johnny was stunned. "I'm fine. I just finished my soda, but thank you, sir."

"Well, at least the boy has manners. I guess that's why you let him work in your store."

"He's very helpful and good with the customers," Tom replied.

"I'm happy for you, Tom." I paused. "I know you didn't come over here to chit-chat. Anyway, let's cut to the chase, shall we? Come on, boy, spit it out. What do you need from me, Johnny?"

"Do you know anything about the cave behind the Parkers' house at the top of the mountain?" Johnny asked.

I rolled my eyes and scrunched my face. I wanted to explode. I shot him a quick grin and gathered my wits. "I like that, a young man who isn't afraid to ask the tough questions. I'm impressed, Johnny." I said, and he returned a nod.

Since he was brave enough to get to the point, I decided to be honest. "Yes, I know about the cave. Tom and I played there when we were kids. Then Tom told me this cockamamie story about you boys finding the cave, human remains, and ghosts." I chuckled. "So, I had to check it out for myself. And much to my surprise, it was all true, just as Tom had described it, including the remains," I said.

Tom and Johnny's mouths were agape, so I continued, "I was thrilled this was not one of Tom's fantasies. I dug up the remains, placed them into a duffle bag, and made my way back down the mountain, stuffed everything into the trunk of my car, and went straight to the cemetery. I figured whoever this person was deserved a better place to rest than a dusty old cave. So I buried them," I said.

"It was Jacob," Johnny chimed in.

"Who's Jacob?" I asked.

"According to the old legends, he's the factory worker who had an affair with Annabelle, Donald Thornhill's wife," Johnny said.

"Interesting," I managed to say through gritted teeth. I was pissed. I would have never moved his remains if I had known it was that guy. I was sure my great-great-grandpa would be pissed at me. "Ah hell, the last thing I wanted to do was help that poor sap." I sighed.

"But you did, which was nice of you," Johnny said.

"I want you to know that Jacob crossed over, which greatly upset Annabelle. You should take some comfort in that," Johnny added.

"Stop it. I don't believe in ghosts," I barked and stared at Tom. *Yes, I did take comfort in knowing this upset Donald's cheating wife.*

"I'm telling the truth," Johnny said, and Tom nodded in agreement.

"Well, if ghosts do exist, then prove it… make one appear right now. If you can't, it's time for you to go."

"It's not that easy, and I'm sure you know that." Johnny was growing frustrated. "Jimmy, can you hear me? Please, Jimmy, I need you to show yourself," Johnny begged and looked around the room for any signs of Jimmy.

"So now you're telling me Jimmy's a ghost, too?" I was stunned by this revelation. Tom never mentioned that to me. I guess I couldn't trust him with all my secrets if he didn't share his with me.

A few minutes passed, and Tom and I looked around the room. We saw nothing— no Jimmy… no ghost… no nothing. How disappointing. But it made sense. Jimmy had never been inside my house. Maybe he couldn't come into the house.

"Listen, I'm sure you thought you saw something in the cave that day. I agree it's a spooky place, but whatever you think you saw was a reflection or something like that, not a ghost," I said and shrugged off any notion of ghosts. *I couldn't risk anyone finding out about April and Bobby.*

"I know what I saw. If you have the puzzle box, I'll show you what it showed us," Johnny said in desperation.

"I didn't keep the box—I buried it with the remains in the cemetery," I said, quickly making up a lie.

"Liar," a voice barked from the other side of the room. I watched Tank cower and crawl behind the sofa.

I spun around, but there was no one there. "Who's there?"

An eerie white vapor began to appear. It was coalescing, slowly, into the form of a young man. I took a few steps back and stumbled, landing on the couch. I'd seen this before; the last time was Donald Thornhill, and that was the last person I wanted in my house. Tom quickly sat beside me and laid a hand on my shoulder for comfort. "It's alright, Bob; no one will hurt you. I promise." *I see Tom was playing his part, too. That made me feel a little bit better.*

"This can't be." I rubbed my eyes. *I had to play this up. I didn't want the kid learning about April and Bobby.* "No way, you slipped something into my drink. You had to. This can't be happening. Ghosts don't exist." I trembled; *my performance was suburb.*

Jimmy appeared and floated toward us, then sent a chill across the room, dropping the temperature by about ten degrees. I shivered at the sudden drop. My eyes widened in disbelief. I just got rid of one ghost, and now we had a new one to deal with. The pesky little brat Jimmy had returned.

"You have the puzzle box in your closet," Jimmy said.

"I do not," I replied.

"Don't lie to me," Jimmy roared. "I know things, and I see things you can't imagine. But, since I'm here, Johnny won't need the box to prove that ghosts exist, but don't deny that you have the puzzle box when I know you do."

Johnny had a smug look on his face. I hated these cocky little kids. Jimmy hovered over the couch, gazing at me and Tom. "I need to know where Annabelle's body's buried," Jimmy said matter-of-factly, staring directly at me.

"How, ah… how would I know that?" I stuttered. I had never heard of Annabelle until today, so why would he think I would have the answer?

"You can ask Donald Thornhill."

"Donald, who?"

If a ghost could have a color other than white, Jimmy's face would have turned beet red. "I'm going to go berserk and hurt you if you lie to me again," Jimmy threatened.

"Jimmy, calm down," Johnny said, motioning with his hands, but Jimmy ignored him.

"I'm sorry, I don't know any Donald Thornhill." I whimpered to add to my award-winning performance.

"He's your great-great-grandpa?"

"Ah," I hesitated. "I think so, but I never met him. He died a long time ago."

"Yes, he did. But if you call his name, he will answer. You can ask him where Annabelle's buried. I'm sure he'll tell you."

"Why would he tell me anything? And why is this so important?"

"Tell him if we have her remains, we can help him and Annabelle reunite, just like he always dreamed." Jimmy smirked.

"I-I'm not sure what to say." Jimmy made an interesting point. *If we could place Annabelle's remains next to Donald Thornhill in the cemetery, could all this nonsense end?*

"Don't push your luck," Jimmy hissed. "I'm tired of the games. I didn't like the way you treated me when I was alive. It's time to make up for all your mistakes and find out what we need to know before something bad happens to you or your little dog." Jimmy began to flicker out.

"Jimmy, no need for threats…" Johnny said, but he was gone before he finished. I could sense that Jimmy was frustrated with all the drama between Donald Thornhill and Annabelle.

Johnny looked at me with empathy. I gazed at Tom, then back to Johnny. I was sure they thought I was confused or shocked to have seen a ghost. But to be honest, I was thinking about what Jimmy said. Could we really get rid of Donald Thornhill and Annabelle? Even though I didn't think I'd ever met Annabelle unless she was the woman by the river the night of the awakening. I would take his word that she was part of the spirits that haunted this valley.

"Bob," Johnny said calmly, "you just saw a ghost. It wasn't a trick; it happened. Jimmy's right. We need your help, and only you can do this."

I sat up. My eyes glazed over. Johnny glanced at me, then back to Tom. It was an awkward moment. I wanted to tell Johnny everything, but I kept my mouth shut. I scrunched my nose and cocked an eyebrow at Johnny. Slowly, I turned to Tom. "Do you mind if Johnny waits outside," I whispered in Tom's ear.

Tom paused, stared at Johnny, and gave him a nod for the door. "Johnny, would you mind waiting outside?" Tom asked.

For a moment, I thought Johnny wasn't going to leave. Everyone's hope relied on me to discover where Annabelle's remains were hidden. I wasn't sure I could find out, but I wanted to try. I didn't see where I had much of a choice.

Slowly, Johnny pushed to his feet. "I'm sorry, Mr. Smithers; we didn't mean to frighten you." I nodded. He slid his jacket back over his arm and went to the front door. Johnny stopped for a second to look over his shoulder, then pushed the door open and went outside.

"What were you thinking bringing him here like this?" I said in a harsh tone.

Tom leaned back on the couch. "I didn't tell him everything. He has no idea of all the things you and I have been through the past fifteen years," Tom said with a look of concern. "I want this all to end. I think you do, too?" Tom said.

"I do, but you could have given me a heads up you were bringing him over," I said. Tom could tell I was frustrated.

"I needed you to be surprised, and everything went perfectly. Your reactions were great. Listen, Bob, your secret is safe with me. I would never tell anyone about April or Bobby. You have to trust me; we're family, and we have been friends since we were kids," Tom said and smiled.

"You're right," I said in agreement.

"So, are you going to help?" Tom asked. I raised my hand in front of me to signal I wasn't sure.

"I will think about it, but if I agree, shouldn't we have Gladys here for safety?" I was concerned for my safety.

"I don't think Donald will hurt you. You want to help. And if we can bring her remains to the graveyard and bury her next to him, they should cross over together," Tom said. I could see he was confident this was how it would work.

"What about Jimmy?"

"I don't follow," Tom added.

"How does he cross over?" I asked.

"Johnny mentioned to me that Jimmy wanted to get rid of Thornhill and Annabelle. Once that was complete, he would tell Johnny where to find his remains so Johnny could tell the authorities. Once they recover his body, they can lay him to rest, which should cross him over," Tom said.

"It sounds complicated, but if we are successful, all the evil spirits would be gone. Leaving only April and Bobby for me?" I said.

"That's the plan," Tom said.

I nodded in agreement. "Tell Johnny I'll think about it." I extended my hand, and Tom shook it.

TWENTY-SEVEN

Tuesday, July 27, 1976

I had taken several days to think about my meeting with Tom and Johnny. *I wanted all of this to end, but why must everything rest on my shoulders? What if Donald Thornhill didn't like our plan? Why did I have to do this alone?* I would have felt better if Tom or Gladys could have been by my side.

I wasn't sure where to begin. Everyone at work could tell something was bothering me. I played it off, telling them I had a summer cold. I was not sure they'd bought my story. That's fine. I was just the old hermit who lived alone in the woods. That was fine with me.

I fixed dinner and watched Tank play in the yard. He was a good dog; he never left the property. I think he was grateful for me giving him a home. I cooked out on the grill—a nice trout fillet I had caught Sunday morning. April would have been proud of me. I had become an excellent little housekeeper. My home was always clean, and I learned to do laundry and cook. I was also proud of myself for stepping up to the challenge.

Tank and I finished our meals. I gave him a spoonful of my potatoes and a small piece of the fish, ensuring no bones were in it. I didn't want him choking. I cleaned up and decided to sit on the back porch and watch the stream flow past. It was peaceful and relaxing.

I watched the sun set behind the trees to my west. It was a vibrant orange glow. It gave the illusion that the trees were on fire. Tank sat beside me in the double rocking chair April and I had bought only a few months before she passed. We never had time to sit out here and enjoy the view. I never thought my life would be like this, alone. But I was making the most of it.

As darkness fell, I moved inside to avoid the mosquitoes. I sat on the couch and, in a rare moment, decided not to turn on the television. I sat in silence for an hour. My mind filled with thoughts, too many to count. Then, out of the blue, I decided to call him.

"Donald Thornhill, can you hear me?" I paused and wondered how stupid I must look sitting here talking to myself. "Great-Great-Grandpa. Can we talk?" A cool breeze whipped through the house. I sat up, excited for his arrival, but realized a storm was approaching, and I had left the windows open. I had to admit, the cooler air felt great. I stood up, entered the kitchen, opened the refrigerator, and grabbed a Pepsi. I took the bottle opener and popped the top.

I walked toward the TV, then decided to leave it off. I sat next to Tank and stroked his back. He loved it. "Donald, I can help you and Annabelle be together for all eternity," I said, and I chuckled on the inside. "You must think I'm crazy, don't cha boy?" I rubbed Tank's belly as I smiled at his face. *Who knew how much joy I would receive from a dog*? Enjoying the soft cushions, I leaned back in my chair. Another cold breeze ripped through the house. I jumped in my chair when I noticed Donald Thornhill sitting opposite me in the recliner. I was shocked. No dramatic entrance? Yet there was a chill in the air, and it was not coming from outside. Much to my surprise, Tank remained calm.

"You said you wanted to help me?" Donald said in a calm voice.

My heart pounded in my chest; my breath felt short. Either I was having a heart attack or a panic attack. I wasn't expecting him to appear. Yet here he was, sitting directly across from me and speaking like a normal adult. "Hi," I managed to say. I was sure he didn't come here to hear me say hi.

"I'm sorry. I didn't expect you," I said, a hint of panic in my voice.

"Why not? You invited me here, didn't you?" Donald asked.

"Yes, yes I did," I replied.

"Well then, here I am, so tell me why you needed to talk," Donald said, crossing his arms and making direct eye contact.

"Well, we had an idea." I explained everything Johnny and Tom explained to me, doing my best not to leave out any details. I explained why this would work. All I needed was the location of where he buried Annabelle's remains. I watched his reaction closely. He stroked his chin with his fingers and thumb before gently lowering them and rubbing his hands together.

I could tell I piqued his interest; he sat, not saying a word. I watched as the minutes rolled past. "How do I know I can trust you?" he asked.

"We're family; you never turn your back on family," I said sincerely.

"Hum," he whispered. He was giving this a lot of thought and consideration. *I guess that was what made him a successful businessman—that and the fact that he and his family had money. I wondered what happened to all his money after he died. Could a lot of money be hidden in the Parker residence's walls?* I observed him, studying his every move. He seemed so calm, not like the last time we met.

"You need to write this down," Donald said, breaking the silence. I stood, walked to the kitchen drawer, and pulled out a tablet and ink pen before returning to my seat. I was impressed with Tank, lying beside me, watching Donald, and not barking or hiding.

Donald began to tell me about the events of that evening. He had returned home after being in the factory, and he lost his temper when he saw Annabelle with her arms around another man. Donald said he became furious, but he never meant to hurt her. He lost his temper and took it out on the young man, Jacob. He said he couldn't stop. Something had come over him, a feeling he had never felt before. Jealousy was evil, and he didn't stop. He couldn't stop. When he realized what he had done, he tried to cover things up. He carried Jacob into the mountains and buried him in a cave he had found once while hunting.

When he returned home, he was shocked to find Annabelle had hanged herself. He became distraught and once again lost his cool. Donald did what he thought was right. He carried her body into the woods and buried her in their favorite place, where they used to picnic before marriage. He told me step-by-step how to find this location, what to look for, and where to dig to find her remains. He said he wanted nothing more than to spend his life with her, which is why he was telling me all of this. He wished me luck and told me he would do his best to protect me and the others until this was over. Then he said thank you and evaporated before my eyes.

Tank raised his head, looked up at me, then back to the chair. "It's alright, boy," I said, patting his back and rubbing his belly. I looked at the notes I had taken. This guy was only trying to protect his family and lost everything in a fit of rage. That one moment of stupidity… I knew the feeling. Some way, somehow, he and I had lived the same life. We lost everything that mattered to us: our family.

TWENTY-EIGHT

Thursday, July 29, 1976

I spent the past two days dwelling on my chat with Donald Thornhill. He appeared to care about what I had to say. We made a connection. At least, that is what I was hoping we had done. My first impression of him was pure evil. I might have jumped to the wrong assumption. If the information he shared with me was accurate, I could say I was wrong about Donald.

I wasn't sure if I should go check things out alone or pass the information along to Tom and the kids. I would have to give that a little more thought. My boss could tell I was distracted today at work. I lied, saying I wasn't feeling the best. They let me come home early. I swung by the General Store and talked to Tom a little. I told him nothing yet, buying me a bit more time.

Tank was happy to see me when I got home. He was constantly bouncing up and down just inside the door. Of course, I rubbed on him a little and let him out to play in the yard. I unpacked my lunch box and cleaned everything, thinking I might lie on the couch and nap. Just as I got comfortable, Tank started scratching at the door. I sighed and stood, letting him back inside, then resumed my position on the couch.

I woke up hours later. I guess I needed the rest. I only hoped I would be able to sleep that night after such a long nap. I decided on breakfast for dinner again, followed by a bit of television. Darkness fell when I thought I heard something coming from my bedroom. I was pretty sure it was Tank. I sat up and leaned forward. Tank was lying on the floor under the table. Maybe he got tired of looking for scraps and fell asleep right there.

I leaned forward and peered down the dark hallway. Something was going on. I noticed a set of twinkling lights; I rose to my feet. *Was Donald coming back to talk?* "Donald," I muttered. The lights grew brighter and began to take shape as they moved forward. I smiled; I could spot April's body shape a mile away. "Hi," I said, choking a little. I coughed into my hand and gave it another try. "It's great seeing you," I said. April smiled in return. "You haven't visited in a long time. I missed you."

"I can't stay long." April paused. "It puts a drain on me when I appear, but we need to talk," she said. Her voice was soft and sounded the same. She hadn't changed one bit. She wore the same outfit she had on for Bobby's tenth birthday. It'd been fifteen years, and she hadn't aged, yet you could tell the past fifteen had taken a toll on me. My hair was gray, and I had bags under my eyes and wrinkles on my face. I could see the age difference now. She would have turned fifty this year if she had survived the crash.

"What brings you here today?" I wiped a tear from my eye.

"I spoke with Donald, and he told me about the plan. It might work, but it will be dangerous," April warned me.

"I know that, but if it can help restore peace in the valley, then I should give Tom and the kids the information so they can end this. After all, they opened the spirit world," I said as I sat on the couch, watching April float a few feet before me.

"You need to help them. They can't do it alone," April added.

"I'm not helping those kids. Anyway, they don't deserve my help," I said, noticing Tank under the table with one eye open, watching me.

"Stop blaming these kids for what happened to Bobby and me. The tone in her voice was elevated.

"If it wasn't for James Jones and his drinking," I said and breathed deeply, "you and Bobby would still be here, so don't ask me to help them," I said firmly. "That's the last thing I'm going to do."

"Bob Eugene Smithers," April scolded me, placing her hands on her hips. "You know what happened that night, and you need to stop blaming everyone else," April added. I could tell she was pissed. She was acting like this was my fault. Everyone knew differently. I knew differently.

"What are you saying, April?" I said, waiting for her response. "Come on, say it!" I yelled. I watched April soften, her eyes welling up with tears.

"Bob, please don't." She drifted over, sat next to me, and placed her hand on my knee.

I jumped at first. Her hand was freezing. She lifted it slightly. "Sorry, I forgot." She softened a little more. "Bob, it hurts me to remind you. I hope you know that, but it was you that night."

"What do you mean, me?" I said, interrupting harshly. "How dare you accuse me of this!" I waved my hands at April, pointing out she was a ghost, but she already knew that.

"Bob, do you remember what happened the night Bobby and I died?" April asked.

"Of course I do. Do you think I could forget? I've lost so much sleep, mulling everything over and over in my head. Night after night that turned into weeks and months," I said and huffed. "You're blaming me? You know I did everything I could to avoid the other car, the drunken driver, need I remind you. The kid who should never have been drinking and driving. How could he be so reckless? And he didn't even get jail time. There was no justice. The system failed." Tears welled, as did my anger. "I hate that boy and all the kids around here. They took you and Bobby from me. They took everything that ever mattered to me!" I screamed, wiping the tears from my cheeks. "I didn't do this," I reminded April.

"Oh, Bob." April sighed. "We have different memories of that night." Her eyes drilled through me like a laser. Her voice was calm. "Do you remember the bowling party?" she asked.

"Of course I do. Bobby rolled a nighty-six. That was his highest game ever," I said with a smile.

"What else, Bob?" she waited for my response.

"What are you trying to say, April? Do you think this was my fault? Is that what you are saying?" I was trying not to yell. But this conversation was upsetting, and I didn't know why she felt I was to blame. Some way or somehow, she felt this was my fault. I wouldn't say I liked her insinuation. I didn't understand how she could think that I did this.

"Bobby, I told you to wait," April said.

I snapped out of my anger. "Bobby?" I was stunned to see him. I couldn't believe he was floating next to his mother. He showed himself only a few times over the years. "Oh, Bobby, I miss you so much. I'm sorry for everything, and I'm sorry for not spending more time with you. I should have played catch more, and taken you camping and fishing," I said, pausing to catch my breath. I wiped tears from my face. It was great seeing him. "I love you, Bobby. I love you both." I gazed at each one of them.

"Dad, I miss you too." Bobby smiled at me. "Please stop blaming the kids in this town for what happened. You need to help them, please." Bobby was firm and direct.

"You don't understand, Bobby. It's complicated." I tried to muster up a smile.

"No, it's not. These kids didn't take my life. You did," Bobby said, wanting to cry, but he stood firm before his mother and me.

"What are you talking about, Bobby?" I was stunned by his accusation. "I did everything I could to avoid the other car." I waved my hands around, baffled by his comment.

"Dad, why did you drink beer at my birthday party?" Bobby muttered. April laid her hand on his shoulder to comfort Bobby.

I opened my mouth, and no words escaped. I sighed and sank into my seat. I thought back to the night of the accident. *I didn't drink. Let me see,* I searched in my mind, and a vision appeared. *The kids were bowling. I watched Bobby pick up a spare. The parents who stayed at the party talked at the back tables, laughed, and had pizza. I ordered two pitchers of beer and a few mugs for everyone. I was sure Dave's father would drink some. Joey, Mitch, Judy—none of the parents wanted to drink. I remember Helen telling me this was a kid's party. She asked me what I was thinking. I had already paid for the beer. I wasn't about to let it go to waste. I remembered I finished every drop. How could I do that? This was Bobby's tenth birthday, and I was getting drunk. I knew once I got started, I wouldn't stop. Why hadn't I remembered that sooner?*

I looked at Bobby. "You're right. This was my fault," I managed to say. I cupped my hands over my face and pushed my hair back. "Oh my gosh." *I didn't remember turning the wheel.* It was all flooding back to me now. I must have blocked it out. *How could I have been so stupid?*

My shoulder froze. I lowered my hands and noticed Bobby touching me. "It's okay, Dad. We all make mistakes," Bobby said. I stared at him, then at April, and back to Bobby.

"How did you get so smart?" I said, trying to hug him, but I had to catch myself from falling to the floor. A warmth rushed over me. It's one of those proud moments you get when you realize your child is growing up. Even though Bobby would never grow older, he still impressed me.

"He continues to amaze me, too," April added. "So do you, Bob." She smiled down at me.

"Me?" I said, confused.

"Yes, it's been almost fifteen years, and you haven't touched one drop of beer since that night. Or any type of alcohol. We are both proud of you," April said. They both smiled. And I smiled back, trying to hold back the tears.

"I have to go. I grow weak," Bobby said and slightly faded. "I love you, Dad" were the last words Bobby said to me.

"Bobby?" I said. My breathing grew heavy. I clutched my chest. I frantically looked around, but he was gone.

"He'll be fine, dear. He's in his room taking a nap." April smiled. "You can always go lie next to him. He spends a lot of time there," April added.

Her words calmed me. "Thank you. I didn't know that." I gazed at this astonishing woman before me. "I hope you and Bobby show up more often," I mentioned.

"We will try, but first, I need you to help me," April said.

"Was that you in the bathroom… writing help me on the mirror? You know I would do anything for you," I said.

"Yes, that was me. Now, I need you to help Tom and those boys," April said.

"I'm not sure I can," I replied.

"Even after everything you've learned? You and the boy had both been drinking that night. I think you turned in the wrong direction, making the impact worse than it may have been. But we will never know, and it's not worth dwelling on. It's all in the past. It would be best if you let go and move forward. Bobby and I have, and we forgive you," April said with a friendly smile. I think she was flirting with me, and I smiled back.

"Once you help them, Annabelle and Donald will cross over. Jimmy promised to do the same. That will leave Bobby and me. The three of us, just like it was meant to be," April said.

I pondered what she was saying. "Okay, I'll tell Tom and help them, too. I'm unsure what more to do, but I will offer my assistance," I said.

April smiled. I could tell she was delighted, and that made me happy. "Thank you," she whispered. "I hate to leave you, but I need to rest. I'm going to lie in bed and take a nap. Be safe, my love, and make me proud," April said and blinked out.

"April?" Ah, crap, I hate it when they leave. "I love you too," I said, accepting April's invitation. I stood and went to the bedroom to lie next to April.

TWENTY-NINE

Sunday, August 1, 1976

I woke to the sound of birds chirping outside. Tank nestled at my feet. I had decided to make this a long weekend. I called in sick Friday and spent most of yesterday at the house. This allowed me the much-needed time to reflect on everything April, Bobby, and I discussed on Thursday. The mind was a powerful tool; it could bring brilliant ideas into the world and block out bad memories when needed. I was having difficulty processing the fact that I drank on Bobby's birthday. The accident was just as much my fault as it was the fault of James Jones, the boy driving the other car. Yet, Bobby and April found a way to forgive me and be happy with their lives. I guess spirits had feelings, too. I learned new things daily.

I forced my way out of bed, deciding it was time to get up and join the living. That meant getting ready, grabbing something to eat, stopping by the General Store, and visiting Tom. I was glad I had taken notes the night Donald and I had spoken. I was also surprised that he hadn't shown up since, to ask why I hadn't helped yet. I guess he was a patient man. I was thankful for that.

I walked Tank to the door to let him out, allowing him ten to fifteen minutes before bringing him back inside. I rubbed his brown fur and tossed him a doggy bone. "You're such a good boy," I said. His tail wagged like he knew what I was saying.

I grabbed my keys, shut the door, and strolled to the car. The engine roared to life, and I saw Tank peering out the living room window. His face made me smile. I pulled the car onto Lizardville Road. I was the typical Sunday driver, going as slowly as possible and enjoying all the sights. I know; I have seen them a thousand times. The water gently flowed down the creek, dotted with light ripples and white caps in the rapids. I truly lived in a paradise with the surrounding trees, forest, and wildlife. I rounded the final bend. Tom's General Store came into view. I drove to the far side, and I didn't see any sign of Johnny. Maybe he wasn't working— good for me. I parked the car and locked the doors—just a habit.

I started walking toward the front door and noticed an enormous crow perched in the tree as I rounded the corner. Its beady eyes fixed on my every step. I paused, turned, and made a growling face. The crow didn't flinch. But I felt better for trying. I opened the doors to the ring of the bells. "Tom, you here?" I hollered.

"Back here," Tom answered from his office.

I strolled behind the counter and pushed the door open. Tom sat in his chair, working on a stack of invoices. "Sorry to intrude," I said.

"That's fine. I could use a break," Tom said, motioning me to take a seat.

"I won't take much of your time," I said, pulling the folded sheet of paper from my pocket and sliding it across the desk to Tom. I watched as he unfolded the sheet. His eyes darted from side to side. A minute later, his head looked up over the page.

"Is this where she is located?" Tom whispered.

"Why are you whispering?" I said, giving Tom a confused look, then cracking a smile and chuckling lightly. "Yes, that is what he told me. I wrote everything down just as he described it," I added.

"Were you afraid?" Tom asked.

"Just a little at first, but he softened when he heard everything I had to say," I said. "He seemed interested and thrilled to help in any way he could. Thank you for asking me to help. Please don't tell the kids I helped," I said, giving Tom a nod.

"Why not? We're all fighting the same battle," Tom replied.

"All right, I guess, but not a word about April and Bobby." My tone was harsher than expected. "Sorry. Hey, on another note, can we go back fifteen years to the night of the accident?"

"Ah, sure," Tom said, tilting his head quizzically.

"Did the doctor ever tell you that he smelled beer on me or that I had been drinking?" I asked, not hesitating because I needed to know if what April and Bobby said was correct. I just needed to confirm they were right.

Tom opened his mouth, then waved a finger at me. "Dang it, man; I don't remember," Tom said, trying to avoid the question.

"Please don't lie to me. I need to hear it from you," I said, almost begging to learn the truth.

"I think the ambulance driver mentioned something like that. Maybe the surgeon and one of the nurses." Tom bowed his head.

"Why didn't you ever tell me?" I asked.

"Bob, you had lost everything that night. Even the police agreed. That's why no charges were ever filed," Tom said and frowned.

"Does April's mom and dad know this?" I asked.

"I think they did," Tom said as he looked away.

"That explains why they never talk to me," I said.

"Look for a positive, Bob. You have been sober for almost fifteen years. That's something to be proud of," Tom said with a smile.

"Thank you for being honest with me. I appreciate that," I said, pushing the chair back to stand. "One more thing, when do you and the kids plan to move the remains?"

Tom thought for a minute. "I think the earliest would be next weekend. I'll check with Johnny later today, but if we get her, we need to move her the same day," Tom said.

"Let me know if I can help in any way," I added, pushing the chair back where it belonged. I turned and walked to the door. "Thank you," I said and walked back to the car.

April and Bobby were right. This was all my fault. The only thing I could do now was to help restore peace in the valley by getting rid of Annabelle and Donald.

THIRTY

Saturday, August 7, 1976

Tom called me earlier this week and confirmed they would check things out on Saturday. As each day passed and we came closer to the day, I grew nervous. What didn't make sense was that I had already done this once—moving Jacob's body. *So, what was different this time?* These ghosts, or at least Annabelle's, would be putting up a fight, and everyone knew it.

I had only agreed to help because April and Bobby needed me to. I wanted, or more like needed, to keep them safe, and Tom promised no one would know about them if we pulled this off. The time had arrived. The kids should be gathering and making their way up the mountain. Tom and Gladys were tagging along to offer protection. I felt the stones in my pocket and knew it was time to head to the cemetery and begin digging her hole. If everything went according to plan, we would get her in the spot, drop her remains into the hole, cover her up, and then she should cross over. Donald told me that was all he wanted. I hoped that was true. So, if he was correct, he would cross over as well. Let's hope he was right.

I ruffled Tank's fur, showing him the love he deserved. He'd been an awesome dog. My heart raced. I was excited, yet my stomach was twisted in knots. I had an uneasy feeling about this. Too many things could go wrong, and someone or all of us could get hurt or even worse. I rose, and Tank followed me to the door. "Not today, boy." I stroked him a few more times and closed the door behind me. I grabbed my shovel, pick, bath towel, and canteen and made my way to the car.

The drive was quick and easy. *Why was it that when you didn't want to do something or go somewhere, you arrived quickly? But it took forever when it was somewhere you wanted to go?* I guess that was one of those questions that would go unanswered. I slowed my car and pulled through the black, wrought iron gates to Lizardville Cemetery. I was petrified, to say the least. I felt scared and helpless. I knew we were dealing with powers we didn't fully understand, and anything could go wrong.

The brakes screeched, and I stopped the car in the far back corner of the property. I glanced around and didn't see anyone in sight. That was a good thing for me. A thought crossed my mind. *I could dig the hole and get out of there before everything erupted. But then what if they needed my help? I guess there was no way out of this.*

I opened the trunk, grabbed my gear, and headed to the Thornhill tombstone. I paused for a moment to reflect. I stared at Jacob's spot. You couldn't even tell he was buried there. I glanced right, then left, and started to remove the grass and set the pieces to the side below Annabelle's name.

I didn't know how long this would take or how long Tom and the kids would be, if they even showed at all. *If I went through all of this, they had better show up with her remains.*

Stop it, Bob, and dig. My heart was pounding, and I thought it would leap out of my chest. With every shovel full of dirt, I knew I was getting closer to completing my part. *I bet the kids would be shocked to find me here helping them, unless Tom told them I was doing this for them.* I stopped for a moment's rest and picked up my towel to wipe the sweat from my face and body. *I was getting too old for this kind of work.* That sounded like something I said when I moved Jacob's body. I laughed at my own remark. Living alone would do that to a person. You learned to talk to yourself and occasionally answer your own questions.

My fifteen-minute break came and went. I grabbed the canteen and took a long swig. I wanted to pour some over my head and body, but I didn't have enough to waste, at least not until I was finished digging. I shoved the shovel back into the ground and heaved another load. This was going a little easier than I expected, just like when I dug a hole for Jacob.

I pushed forward and forced myself to keep digging. I turned to see if anyone had entered or was driving by the cemetery. There were times when people would stop to visit loved ones. But over the years, there had been a sharp decline in visitors. I was hoping today was one of those days. I was also thankful the Thornhill plot was in the back of the graveyard, out of sight from the road. I shoved the shovel back into the dirt, time after time. I widened the hole on both ends. I think I was getting close to the four-foot-deep marker. I was almost six feet tall and used my body as a measuring device. With each shovel full of dirt I heaved to the side, I grew exhausted. I paused to take another break, grabbed my canteen, and took a long drink. I coughed and drooled down the front of my shirt. I poured a little water into my hand to wipe my face and the front of my shirt to hide the drool.

I continued until I was comfortable with the hole's depth, width, and length. It wasn't easy getting out. I had to notch a few holes into the side wall. They would serve as little steps to place my shoe, helping to give me the lift I needed to pull myself out of the hole. Now, for the hard part: I sat and waited.

I approached the tree line, perched myself against a large oak tree, then lowered myself to the ground. It was much cooler sitting in the shade. After an hour, I decided to go to the car, lie down, and take a nap until they showed up. At this point, I was plenty rested and just wanted to get this over with. I hoped they would show up soon, toss in the bag, and cover the hole so we could all go home. I was sure Tank needed to go outside before sunset.

I must have dozed off when I heard a commotion. I sat up and noticed two cars making their way to the back of the cemetery. One was Tom's old car. I was glad he didn't drive his Mustang. Another car followed closely behind and was driven by Lexi Parker. I watched as they rolled to a stop near the fence line; the screeching brakes made me cringe.

I watched as they unloaded the cars. The older boys and Gladys climbed out of Tom's vehicle while the younger brats stepped out of the rear car. Gladys was carrying a smoke chamber or something. I could see the smoke rising as she walked toward the burial plot. My heart fluttered. The show was about to start, and I wasn't sure how things would play out. I had this uneasy feeling that something was about to go wrong, especially since everything had gone as planned up to this point. The sun was setting, and the temperature was dropping. We were in for a lovely, cool evening. Mother Nature was doing her part.

I sat up, watching Tom, Gladys, and the kids walking through the tall grass. It was darker than I expected. I looked at my watch; it wasn't that late. The shadows from the trees must have created the illusion of being dark.

The setting was perfect for a funeral. The group made their way into the graveyard. The boys stopped to look at several of the headstones. *We didn't have time for this. Come on, Tom, get them to hurry up. They needed to understand the urgency of the situation.* I opened my door and approached Tom, who turned and waited for me to catch up.

Lexi, Sara, Scooter, Johnny, and Todd walked behind Tom, Gladys, Buck, and Parker. Those were the real troublemakers. I did a quick headcount, and there were ten of us all together. That made me feel more at ease, even though I'd seen these otherworldly powers. If Annabelle was a scorned woman, then look out; we could be in trouble.

I walked over and extended my hand to Tom's. "Good to see you, my friend," I said.

"Nice seeing you, too. I'm glad you made it," Tom said and gave me a wry smile.

"Thank you for asking me to help. Now, can we get this over with?" I smirked.

"I agree. I don't like this place and don't want to be here when darkness falls," Tom replied. I was in total agreement with Tom. I didn't want to be here, either. I was standing in the back of Lizardville Cemetery, looking at all the grave markers. *Who knew how many ghosts roamed this place?* The hairs on my arm stood up. I spotted a few bats taking flight from the trees. The lightning bugs flickered in and out in the surrounding fields. The crickets chirped, and nightfall was upon us.

I pointed to an enormous headstone. We walked in that direction until the stone was before us. From everyone's expression, the name on the right side of the stone was shocking. DONALD THORNHILL WAS A LOVING HUSBAND, FATHER, AND BUSINESS OWNER. 1858-1904. Wow, he was only forty-six. He looked much older than that when we'd met.

Another name was carved in the middle of the large rock: ANNABELLE THORNHILL, A LOVING WIFE AND MOTHER. 1879-1904. She was only twenty-five. I stood in silence, as did the others. I knew her remains were not in this spot that bore her name. I paid no attention to this before. The third name on the left side was ELIZABETH THORNHILL, A LOVING DAUGHTER FROM 1900-1972. My jaw dropped open—she had been alive in recent years, and I had no idea. I didn't think any of us had realized that. She was most likely the last person put to rest in this cemetery. I would have been related to her in some odd way.

That's when the kids and Tom noticed the gaping hole I had dug in front of Annabelle Thornhill's grave marker. All we had to do was put the remains of Annabelle into the hole and cover her up. Donald would be at peace because his wife had returned to where she belonged. Annabelle would be beside her husband and daughter, and with any luck, they would all cross over.

I glanced right and left. "Hey Tom, where's the body?" I asked.

Tom didn't get a chance to answer. We were startled by a loud commotion in the trees to our left. A chilling blast of wind raced across the field. I cursed under my breath. *I knew things were going too smoothly.* I assumed the female ghost was Annabelle, who had roared out of the trees. Her high-pitched screams rattled our senses. We dropped to our knees and covered our ears to muffle the sound. Quickly, another translucent figure bolted from the woods—Donald Thornhill. He pointed in her direction, and I spotted a light beam shooting from his finger directly at Annabelle. I couldn't believe what I was witnessing. Annabelle spun around and waved her hand, deflecting his shot. With a swipe of her hand, a large beam of light flashed across the field, hitting Donald and sending him tumbling back to the tree line.

The screaming stopped. I turned to find many of the others hiding behind the tombstones. I darted and dove behind a large monument to shield myself from the fight that was taking place before my eyes. I glanced over the top of the rock to find Gladys standing in the wide-open space next to the open grave site. She was chanting and waving the canister from side to side. She didn't appear to be afraid at all. Maybe it was the stones that protected her. Perhaps the smell the smoke was putting off as it continued to pour out of the canister made her feel safe in the middle of the ghostly fight.

I gripped the edge of the headstone and peered over the top—a flash of light shot to the right; another shot back to the left. This was unbelievable, something you would only see at the movies. Two blurry, incandescent light figures were fighting before my eyes, both determined to defeat the other. Swishing and a whooshing, they beamed around in a blur.

I didn't know what I was thinking. *Was I brave or stupid?* But I got to my feet and darted toward Tom's car. As I ran past Tom, he rose and followed closely behind. The battle moved closer in the direction of Tom's car. I stopped short of the vehicle. Tom fumbled in his pocket for the keys. He finally grabbed them and tried to insert them into the truck to get it open. Annabelle noticed what we were doing and made a beeline for Tom. Just like that, she was standing between us. She let out a scream that sent us to our knees. I rolled to one side and covered my ears.

It was her, the night of the awakening… The woman I spotted next to the river. It was Annabelle! She'd been to my house. April never mentioned that.

As I rolled on the ground, thinking this would be how I would die, I noticed Johnny approaching us. I was not sure what he was thinking. I grabbed the stones in my pocket and realized they were doing me no good. I wished I had thought to fill my pockets with salt. Johnny took cover behind the last gravestone at the edge of the cemetery. Annabelle stood firm, continuing her rage. She kept Tom and me paralyzed with her scream. Simultaneously, with one hand stretched out, she pointed at Donald, who appeared to be in the exact location. *How long could a person—okay, so she's not technically a person—well, how long could a ghost scream?* I wondered.

I was not sure when I noticed the stones flying in our direction. I didn't want to get hit by one of them, and I didn't want Tom's car to get hit. Then, one of the rocks passed directly through Annabelle. She appeared stunned and stopped screaming. Her outstretched hand fell to her side, and she turned to face the kids. "Aw, crap!" I yelled.

I uncovered my ears as I lay on the freezing ground. I tried to force myself to my feet. Tom was doing the same.

Tom slid the key into the truck, and the lid sprang open. I grabbed one side of the duffle bag, and Tom grabbed the other side. We pulled it from the car and started walking in the direction of her grave, soon to be her final resting place. I noticed Johnny glancing in our direction. I frantically pointed toward Annabelle, but Johnny wasn't paying attention. She waved her hand, sending a brilliant flash of light directly at Johnny. It sent Johnny flying a few feet into the air. I hoped he was alright. *How could a ghost do that?* I didn't know they could hurt the living. I guess I was wrong.

I spotted the petite girl, Sara, and her older sister, Lexi, running toward Johnny. Tom and I continued our trek toward the open hole. The bag was heavier than I expected. I heard one of the girls yelling. *Oh crap, that can't be good. Had Annabelle killed him*? This ghost was getting on my nerves, and I was not going to have any of this. I noticed Buck racing to his brother's side.

Tom and I increased our speed to the open hole when my foot got caught in a patch of weeds. I tripped, falling face-first to the ground. The duffle bag flew out of my hand, and Tom was jerked backward and fell on his butt. We hurried to get to our feet, grabbed the handle, and started moving forward. "Duck!" I yelled to Tom, as I threw my body to the ground. Tom got down just as a beam of light soared over his head. Annabelle had more power than any of us could have imagined. I think she was even more formidable than Donald Thornhill. Or was Donald holding back because he loved her so much? *That had to be it. The things people would do for the ones they loved*!

Tom grabbed hold of the green bag and started crawling on his hands and knees. The load was too heavy for one person. I followed suit and began to crawl. I grabbed the other handle, and we inched our way closer to the open grave. *If we only had a way to distract Annabelle, that would give us the time we needed to make it the rest of the way. This could all be over.*

I think the kids were reading my mind or something. I spotted Parker, the new guy Todd, and Buck. It looked like they were running some sort of football play. Parker dashed in one direction; simultaneously, the new guy went up the middle while Buck and Johnny flanked to the right. They all broke and started running toward Annabelle. It put a smile on my face to see Johnny was all right. I didn't want anyone to get hurt or even worse.

If this worked, they would all reach her at about the same time. I was unsure what they would do when they got to Annabelle. *How do you tackle a ghost?* But if anything, it should keep her busy long enough for Tom and me to reach our destination. Tom pushed forward and got to his feet, as did I. Our pace quickened. The hole was in sight. From the corner of my eye, I noticed one of the boys started throwing rocks at Annabelle. He would toss a rock and then duck behind the headstone. All this was buying Tom and me the time we needed to get her remains in the hole.

I noticed Parker was the first to arrive at the floating spirit, and he dove right at her. With the wave of a hand, he was tossed to the side like a sack of potatoes. The new guy reached her and dove, passing directly through her and landing head-first in the dirt below. She staggered backward a little. The new kid quickly turned and tried to scurry away. I would never forget the expression on his face.

He looked terrified. Moments later, Buck arrived, diving through her ghostly presence. Seconds later, Johnny lunged at Annabelle with his whole-body momentum. She spun, making eye contact as if she knew Johnny could hurt her. *Maybe it was some sort of human instinct that kicked in.* I loved the expression on her face as she turned to face her attacker. He passed through her and ended up lying next to the other boys. She looked enraged to think they had a chance of defeating her. It was preposterous to believe they could have fazed her, but their plan worked.

Tom and I were only a few yards away from completing the job. My mind raced, and my heart filled with excitement, knowing this could soon end. Tom and I slowly turned to face Annabelle to show we had won. She thrust her arms forward as a brilliant spark of light sent Tom and me backward several feet. This wasn't the time to gloat. I heard the blood-curdling sound of bones inside the bag as it hit the ground, sending shivers down my spine. I gritted my teeth and tried to force my body to move. I hurt everywhere, and from the expression on Tom's face, so did he. A large white cloud floated over; I sighed a bit, relieved to see it was Donald Thornhill. He slowly hovered over the bag and cast his sight downward. A sad reflection of a once-proud man and factory owner, he loved and cared for his wife. The rejection he was feeling was evident by the look on his face.

Annabelle was winning the battle. She had figured out what we were trying to accomplish. There wasn't much we could do to stop her. She rocketed to the bag and was about to move it away from the grave when a giant flash of light appeared. Stunned and panicked, she recoiled as the light made its way in her direction.

Shaken and out of breath, I watched helplessly only a few feet away as Jimmy bolted onto the scene. He went directly for Annabelle and passed through her in one swift move. She spiraled to the ground and appeared to be unconscious. Jimmy had waited for the perfect time to arrive.

"Move!" Tom yelled.

We found our strength and scrambled to our feet, grabbed a strap on the bag, picked it up, and swung it swiftly. The bag lunged toward the open grave. Bullseye! I watched as the bag tumbled out of sight. Tom and I both smiled as we reached for the shovel, but before Tom could pour the first load of dirt, the shovel was dislodged from his hand by a ray of light. *Now, I wish I had brought two shovels instead of just one. How could I have been so careless? This could be the difference between life and death.*

I glanced up. Annabelle looked petrified, and I watched as she bolted sparks at Tom and in my direction. The kids crawled on their hands and knees to the nearest gravestone and took cover. Tom started kicking dirt in the direction of the hole, trying to start the process of filling the grave as he moved away. Gladys watched as she continued her chant and waved the smoke-filled canister from side to side. I still was not sure if that was doing any good. However, Annabelle never tried to harm her. *Why wasn't she over here protecting the hole along with Tom and me so we could finish this?*

Someone needed to do something. There were too many of us to let Annabelle win. We had to send her to the other side and end this here and now. That's when I noticed Johnny was standing, and he started walking toward Tom and me. I was unsure what he had up his sleeve when Sara began to scream.

"No, what are you doing?" She hollered as she stepped from behind the massive headstone protecting her. Lexi tried to pull her down, but she shook herself free and stepped out front, putting herself in harm's way.

Buck, Parker, and the new boy crawled toward the mound of dirt as Gladys began to walk in a circle around the open hole. She hovered over it and began to chant something. I couldn't make out what she was saying. It may have been in Latin.

Tom and I regained our balance and stood before Annabelle could strike. Jimmy tossed a fireball at her. Or at least that is what it looked like. The impact rocked her back on her heels. Donald approached from her blindside and tackled her to the ground.

I was amazed. I didn't know one ghost could grab another spirit and hold them down. Jimmy spun his hands around in a circle and whipped up a pale-colored rope as he approached Annabelle. Tom and I hurried toward the dirt pile and did everything possible to fill the hole quickly. We used our hands and feet to push the dirt into the open pit. The sound of earth hitting the canvas sack quickly turned to loud thuds as the dirt landed on dirt. Tom used the shovel, and I used my hands like a bulldozer. Now, I wished I hadn't dug the hole this deep. We both stayed focused. Parker and Buck moved in to help push dirt. Johnny ran to the younger girl—bit by bit, the hole started to fill.

Gladys was now walking in a circle around Donald, Jimmy, and Annabelle, surrounding them with smoke and trapping them inside. Annabelle squirmed and kicked, trying to break free, but this time she was overpowered. She let out one more of her screams that forced all of us to cover our ears, but that quickly subsided. We continued to launch dirt into the hole. Annabelle's voice sounded raspy. Her translucent figure started to dissipate. She blinked in and out for a second or two, and her voice faded. Something was happening. I think we were winning.

"Stop. Please stop," Annabelle begged. "Gladys, you're my great-granddaughter. How could you do this to your family, to me? Please." She frowned, stretching her hands outward.

We continued to pile more dirt into the hole. I watched as the soil grew closer to the top. Jimmy floated a few feet away, as did Donald. Annabelle frowned, a tear tracing down her face. Donald smiled. They were both growing lighter. I grappled with what was happening. Our plan was working—she and Donald would cross over and be gone.

Annabelle struggled to stand, casting a look in our direction. "Why…?" Her entire body blinked in and out, and her eyes drooped in defeat. Her face was animated with shock and disgust as tears rolled down her cheeks. "Why?" she mouthed. "Why?" Then, she vanished.

Donald Thornhill stood triumphantly. He hovered off the ground a few feet, taking his place over his grave marker. He bowed toward me, then Tom, and smiled—something I was sure he hadn't done in some time. Casting a look at each of us, he mouthed, "Thank you," before his white mist seeped downward into the ground, and he moved to another world.

My mouth fell open. I glanced around and noticed everyone doing the same. We were all in awe of what had transpired in the cemetery. Tom's mother closed the doors on the side of the canister, and the smoke stopped polluting the air. Tom and I smiled, hugged each other quickly, shook our fists before us, and briefly danced.

We all celebrated, the kids still cheering in the background. When I motioned for Tom to start handing me the large pieces of grass, I started at one end and worked my way to the other, covering every inch to ensure she could not find a way out. Tom and I paced back and forth on the grass to pack it down and level it out.

I brushed off my hands and wiped the dirt from my jeans. I was ready to head home and get a great night's sleep. This whole adventure had worn me out. I glanced around the graveyard and didn't see Jimmy's ghost anymore. I wonder if he would live up to his promise; I didn't know why he wouldn't. I guess time would tell.

The kids were joyous, still jumping up and down in celebration. The boys high-fived each other like they had won the high school state championship in football. Each acted like their role was more important than the others'. They could have all the credit. I was happy and felt a weight had been lifted off my shoulders. I couldn't believe that this plan actually worked and that this was finally over. Annabelle and Donald Thornhill were gone, I hoped.

"Nice job." Tom patted me on the back and started walking toward his car, and I was only a step behind. We both noticed Gladys standing next to the vehicle. I guess she was ready to go, too. It's funny that she never said a word. She waited for Tom to open her door and slid in. What a strange woman. She kept us safe, and I loved her for that. I paused and waited for the boys to walk up and pile into the car. As they passed, I smiled and gave each of them a pat on the back. Tom's engine roared to life, and so did Lexi's. I watched as they rolled away.

I popped my trunk and put the towel inside. *That was a nice green duffle bag. Too bad I had to toss it into the ground. I'd have to stop by the store and pick up another one. That might protect my tools from rust during the winter months.*

I closed the trunk, walked to the driver's side door, and glanced around the cemetery. Everything was peaceful, just like before I had arrived. I sat down, closed my door, turned the key, and drove the car. I checked for traffic. I was not sure why. You never saw cars out here, especially on a Saturday night. I smiled a few times and even giggled once as I drove. This really worked.

My mind whirled, thinking about everything I had seen tonight. The past fifteen years had been filled with so many exciting adventures. Many of them were spooky and life-threatening. I thought back to my last conversation with April. She asked me to help the kids, and I did. I was hoping she would be proud of me. I couldn't wait to see her reaction. My mind drifted to Bobby. Our last conversation was tough. He wanted me to admit fault for the traffic accident. It wasn't easy because I had to remember that night, but he was right. One good thing did come out of it: I was fifteen years sober.

My smile faded. I panicked and pushed the gas pedal to the floor. Annabelle and Donald had crossed over, and Jimmy had promised to do the same. *What if April and Bobby were gone? April requested I help; she was adamant about it. Did she trick me? Was that what held her here? I needed to learn to be a team player and stop hating the kids. I also admitted my wrongdoing to Bobby. Could that be what held him here? How could I be so stupid?*

No, it couldn't be. I was overthinking this. I needed to see April and Bobby. I wanted things the way they used to be—just the three of us.

I pulled into the driveway, parking along the side of the house. I turned the car off and slammed the door behind me as I ran to the house. I pulled the door open, and Tank raced out. Oh man, the little guy was quick and scared me as I scuttled back. It was dark, and I couldn't let him out by himself. There were too many wild creatures that roamed the woods at night. I flicked the light switch, casting a light over the yard, and there he was. He danced around and sniffed here and there before choosing his spot. Finally, he finished, and Tank scampered back to me. I picked him up, hugged him, and carried him into the house. Tank was happy to see me.

I closed the door with my foot, sat Tank on the floor, and then latched the lock. I opened a few windows to get a breeze going into the house. I was feeling a bit warm.

I leaned back on the couch. "April," I said, waiting for a reply. "Bobby," I whispered. "Are you here? Please give me a sign." Anxiously, I waited in silence. Minutes passed. "April? Bobby?" I cried out. "Please! Can you give me a sign?" I whimpered and waited with Tank by my side. I listened to the clock tick as the minutes passed. The minutes turned into hours. *I never got to say goodbye.*

ACKNOWLEDGMENTS

I'm a writer, so I primarily work alone. I greatly appreciate my wife, Toni, for tolerating and putting up with my weird ways and allowing me the time I needed to complete this story. Thank you for being the first to read my work and giving me valuable feedback.

Thank you to 4 Horsemen Publications, Erika Lance, and Valerie Willis for taking a chance on me and allowing me to follow my dreams.

Thank you to Gayle Staggemeyer for finding those elusive mistakes that drive readers up the wall, along with your thoughts and suggestions during editing.

Thank you to my daughter Jessica for working with me on this project. I valued all your suggestions, ideas, and criticism throughout the writing process.

Thank you to all the Alpha readers—Silvia Curry, Carolyn Hornick, Phoenix Whirl, and Teresa Allaert Thompson—for taking time out of your day to read my story and tell me what worked and what didn't.

A special shoutout and thank you to all the readers for your support. I could not do this if it were not for you. You are the best.

BOOK CLUB QUESTIONS

1. What did you think of the writing? Are there any standout sentences?

2. Would you want to read another book by this author?

3. Did you guess the ending? If so, at what point?

4. Which twist surprised you the most?

5. If you could ask the author anything, what would it be?

6. How does the book's title work with the book's contents? What would you choose if you could give the book a new title?

7. Would you ever consider re-reading it? Why or why not?

8. Are there lingering questions from the book you're still thinking about?

9. Did the book frighten you or get under your skin in any way?

10. Which characters did you like best? Which did you like least?

11. Who would you choose if you had to trade places with one character?

12. What did you think of the book's length? If it's too long, what would you cut? If too short, what would you add?

13. What songs does this book make you think of? Create a book group playlist together!

14. Which places in the book would you most like to visit?

15. Did the book strike you as original?

16. What do you think of the book's cover? How well does it convey what the book is about?

17. What other books by this author have you read? How did they compare to this book?

18. Was the pacing— beginning, middle, and end— done well?

AUTHOR BIO

Steve Altier is a bestselling paranormal, mystery, and suspense writer. He is known for his multi-award-winning series, *The Lizardville Ghost Stories*, and *Lizardville Side Stories* series. Steve grew up in a small town in central Pennsylvania. His parents owned the dam keeper's house on Lizardville Road. Across the street was an old, broken-down dam and the remnants of the ax factory.

Steve and his buddies spent many days exploring the abandoned factory. Unexplained things happened when Steve was a child—inspiring his love for everything spooky, along with many of his stories. Steve currently lives in Florida with his wife, four daughters, and four cats.

Learn more about Steve and his work by following him on social media or visiting his website. **www.stevealtier.com**

Steve would love to hear from you. You can email him at **authorstevealtier@outlook.com**

MORE BOOKS FROM
4 HORSEMEN PUBLICATIONS

PARANORMAL & URBAN FANTASY

AMANDA FASCIANO
Waking Up Dead
Dead Vessel
Dead Show
Dead Revelations
Dead Carnage

BEAU LAKE
The Beast Beside Me
The Beast Within Me
Taming the Beast: Novella
The Beast After Me
Charming the Beast: Novella
The Beast Like Me

CHELSEA BURTON DUNN
By Moonlight
Moon Bound
White Moon
New Moon Rising

J.M. PAQUETTE
Call Me Forth
Invite Me In
Keep Me Close

KAIT DISNEY-LEUGERS
Antique Magic
Blood Magic
Heart Magic

LYRA R. SAENZ
Prelude
Sonata
Scherzo
Ragtime Swing
Midnight Cumbia
Sea Song de la Corsaire
Falsetto in the Woods: Novella
The Devil's Trill

MEGAN MACKIE
The Finder of the Lucky Devil
The Saint Liars
The Devil's Day
The Digital Mage

PAIGE LAVOIE
I'm in Love with Mothman
I'm Engaged with Mothman

ROBERT J. LEWIS
Shadow Guardian and the
Three Bears
Shadow Guardian and the
Big Bad Wolf
Shadow Guardian Boys
That Went Woof

VALERIE WILLIS
Cedric: The Demonic Knight
Romasanta: Father of Werewolves

The Oracle: Keeper of the
Gaea's Gate

Artemis: Eye of Gaea
King Incubus: A New Reign

Young Adult Fantasy

C.R. Rice
Denial
Anger
Bargaining
Depression
Acceptance
Broken Beginnings:
Story of Thane
Shattered Start: Story of Sera
Sins of The Father: Story of Silas
Honorable Darkness: Story of
Hex and Snip

A Love Lost: Story of Radnar

Leslie & Janice Sommers
Brighde Reborn
Brighde Redefined

Valerie Willis
Rebirth
Judgment
Death

**Discover more at
4HorsemenPublications.com**

www.ingramcontent.com/pod-product-compliance
Lightning Source LLC
Chambersburg PA
CBHW061523310726
48972CB00008B/2308